Ali Baba and the Forty Thieves

RELOADED

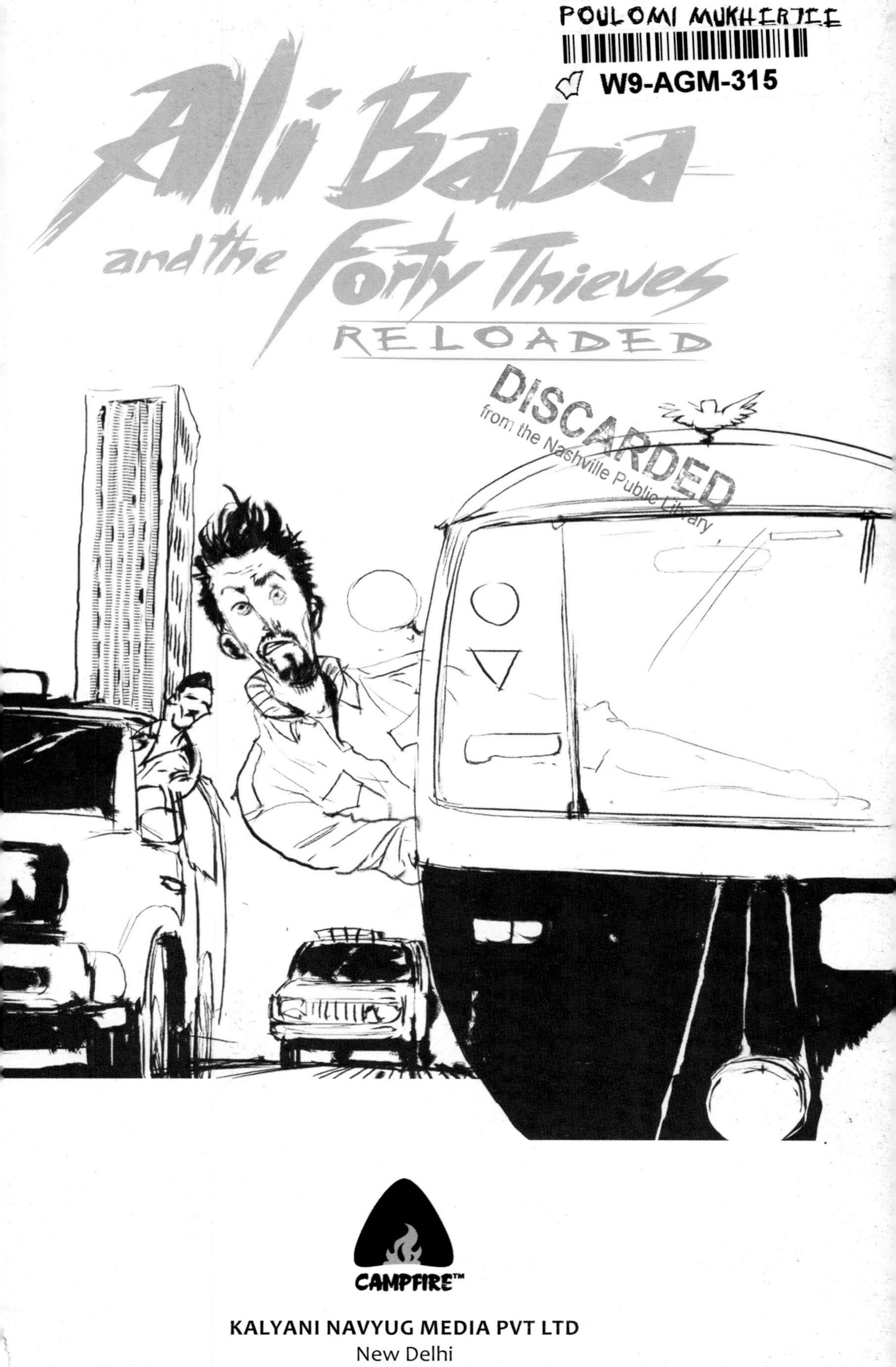

CAMPFIRE™

KALYANI NAVYUG MEDIA PVT LTD
New Delhi

Ali Baba and the Forty Thieves RELOADED

Sitting around the Campfire, telling the story, were:

ILLUSTRATOR **AMIT TAYAL**

COLORIST **AJO KURIAN**

LETTERER **BHAVNATH CHAUDHARY**

EDITORS **ABHIMANYU SINGH SISODIA**

EMAN CHOWDHARY & SUKANYA MEHTA

EDITOR (INFORMATIVE CONTENT) **RASHMI MENON**

PRODUCTION CONTROLLER **VISHAL SHARMA**

ART DIRECTOR **RAJESH NAGULAKONDA**

COVER ART

ILLUSTRATOR **AMIT TAYAL**

COLORIST **AJO KURIAN**

DESIGNER **JAYAKRISHNAN K. P.**

CAMPFIRE™

www.campfire.co.in

Published by Kalyani Navyug Media Pvt. Ltd.
101 C, Shiv House, Hari Nagar Ashram, New Delhi 110014, India
www.campfire.co.in

ISBN: 978-93-80741-13-0

Printed in India at Nutech Photolithographers

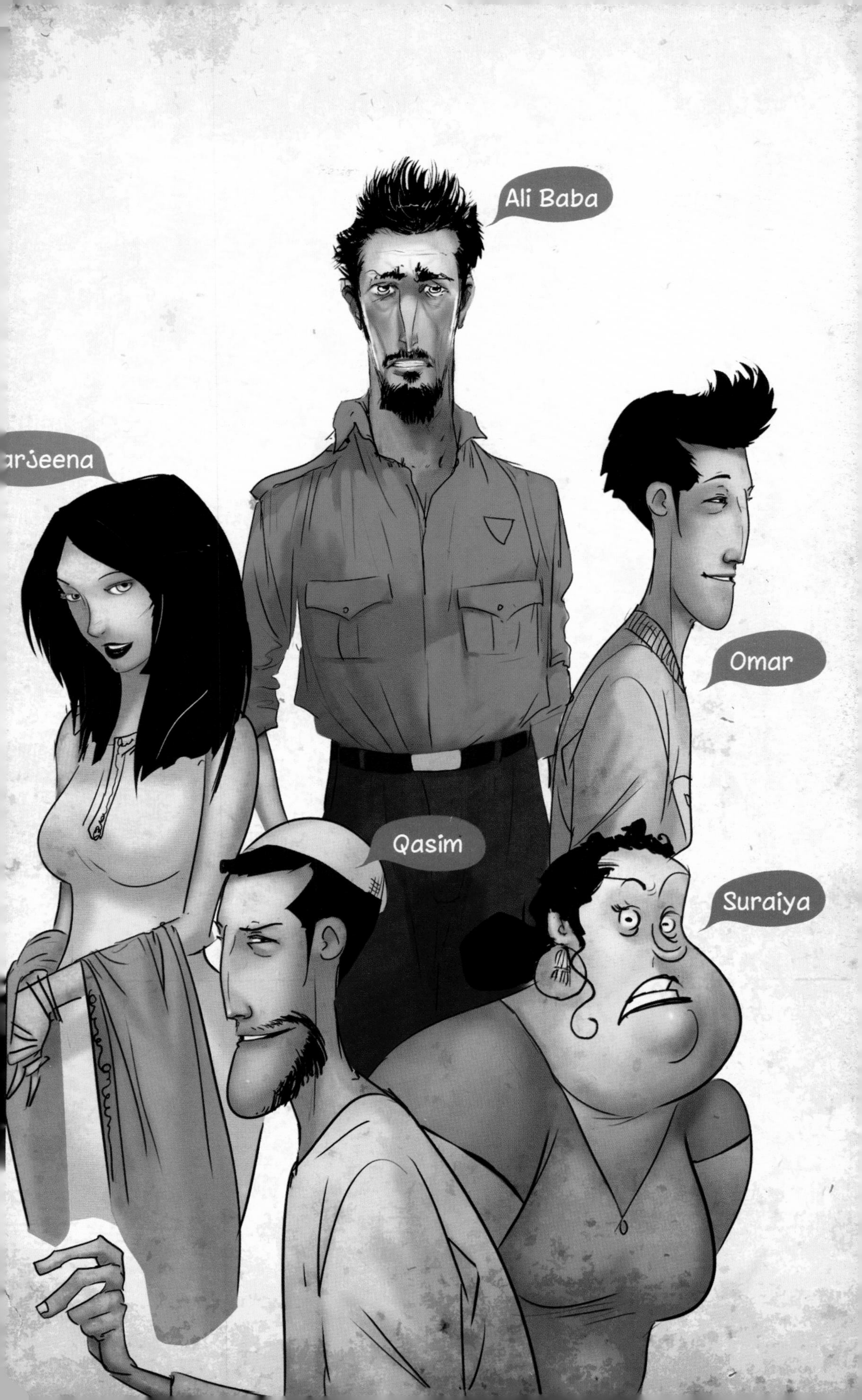
Ali Baba
arJeena
Omar
Qasim
Suraiya

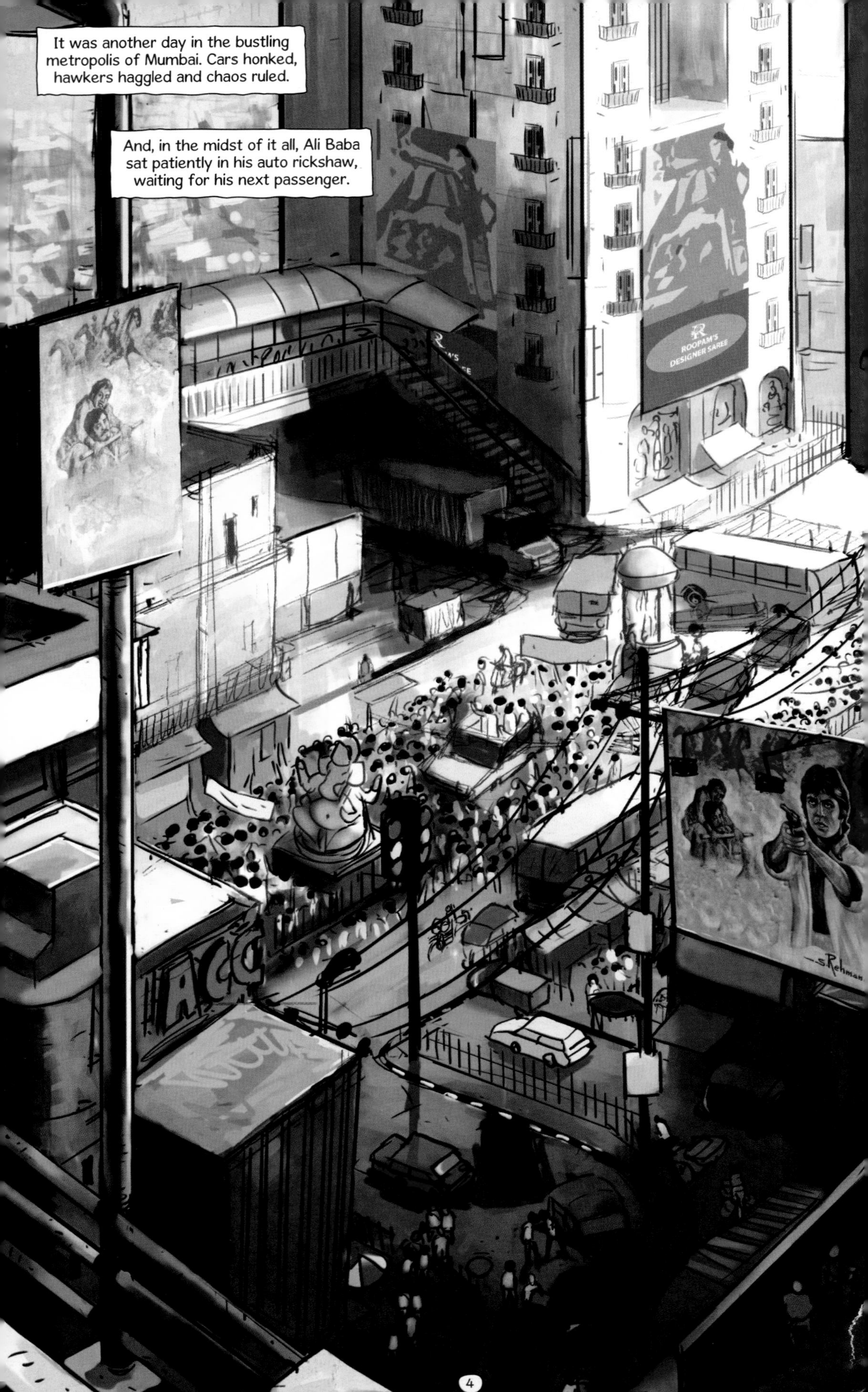
It was another day in the bustling metropolis of Mumbai. Cars honked, hawkers haggled and chaos ruled.
And, in the midst of it all, Ali Baba sat patiently in his auto rickshaw, waiting for his next passenger.
ROOPAM'S DESIGNER SAREE
ACC
S.Rehman

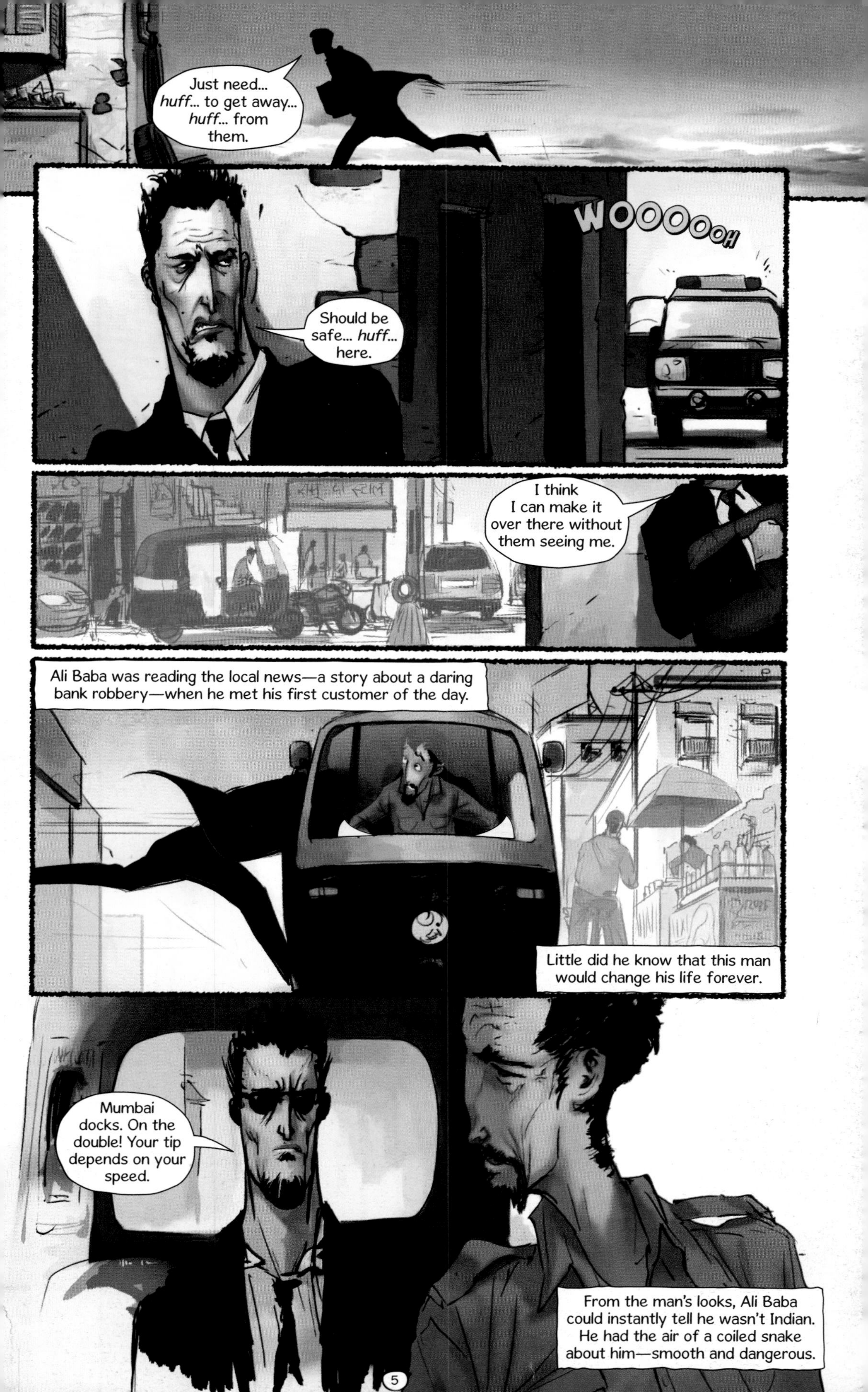

Just need... huff... to get away... huff... from them.
Should be safe... huff... here.
WOOOOOOH
I think I can make it over there without them seeing me.
Ali Baba was reading the local news—a story about a daring bank robbery—when he met his first customer of the day.
Little did he know that this man would change his life forever.
Mumbai docks. On the double! Your tip depends on your speed.
From the man's looks, Ali Baba could instantly tell he wasn't Indian. He had the air of a coiled snake about him—smooth and dangerous.

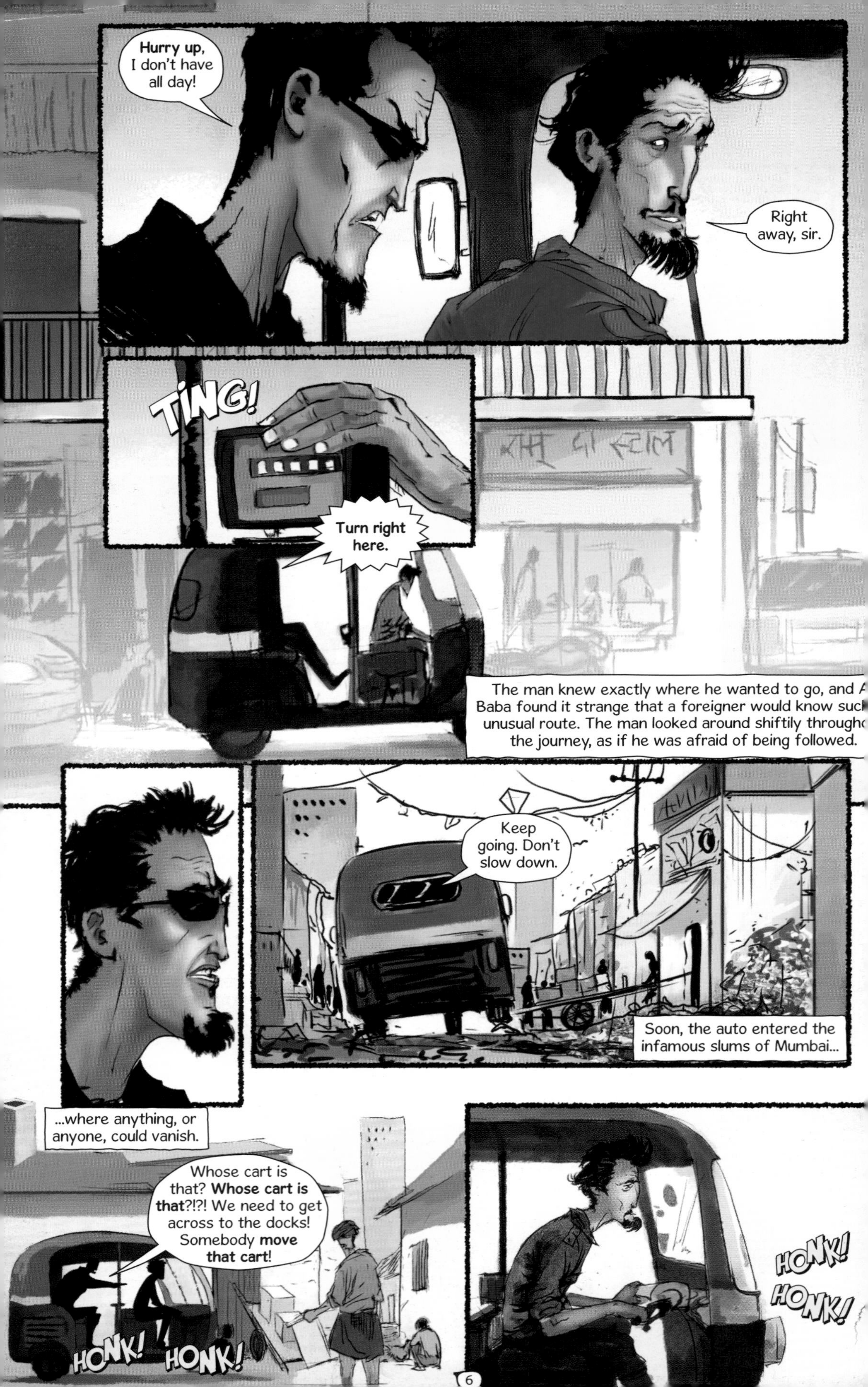
Hurry up, I don't have all day!
Right away, sir.
TING!
Turn right here.
The man knew exactly where he wanted to go, and
Baba found it strange that a foreigner would know suc
unusual route. The man looked around shiftily through
the journey, as if he was afraid of being followed.
Keep going. Don't slow down.
Soon, the auto entered the infamous slums of Mumbai...
...where anything, or anyone, could vanish.
Whose cart is that? Whose cart is that?!?! We need to get across to the docks! Somebody move that cart!
HONK! HONK!
HONK! HONK!

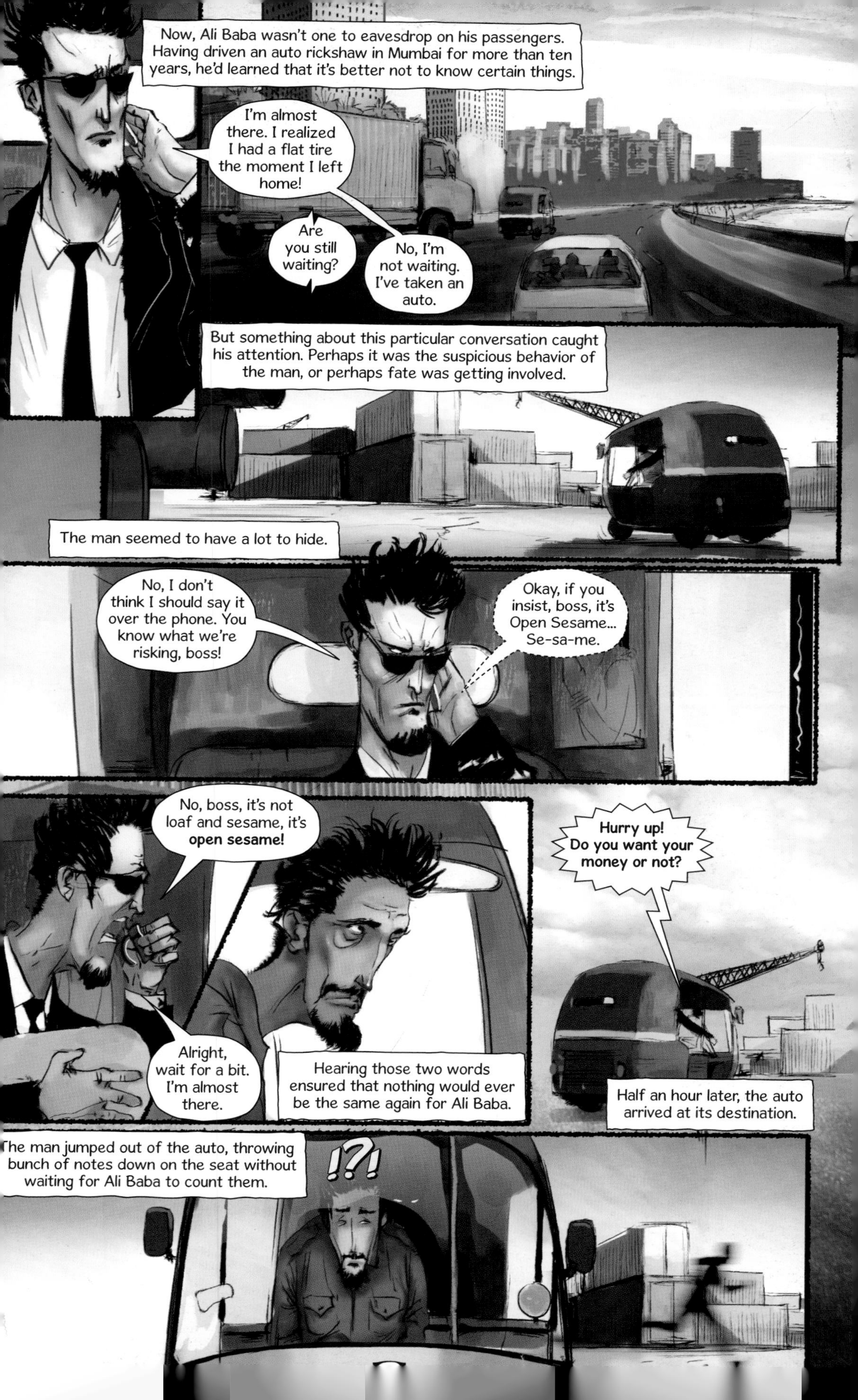
Now, Ali Baba wasn't one to eavesdrop on his passengers. Having driven an auto rickshaw in Mumbai for more than ten years, he'd learned that it's better not to know certain things.
I'm almost there. I realized I had a flat tire the moment I left home!
Are you still waiting?
No, I'm not waiting. I've taken an auto.
But something about this particular conversation caught his attention. Perhaps it was the suspicious behavior of the man, or perhaps fate was getting involved.
The man seemed to have a lot to hide.
No, I don't think I should say it over the phone. You know what we're risking, boss!
Okay, if you insist, boss, it's Open Sesame... Se-sa-me.
No, boss, it's not loaf and sesame, it's **open sesame!**
Alright, wait for a bit. I'm almost there.
Hearing those two words ensured that nothing would ever be the same again for Ali Baba.
Hurry up! Do you want your money or not?
Half an hour later, the auto arrived at its destination.
The man jumped out of the auto, throwing bunch of notes down on the seat without waiting for Ali Baba to count them.
!?!

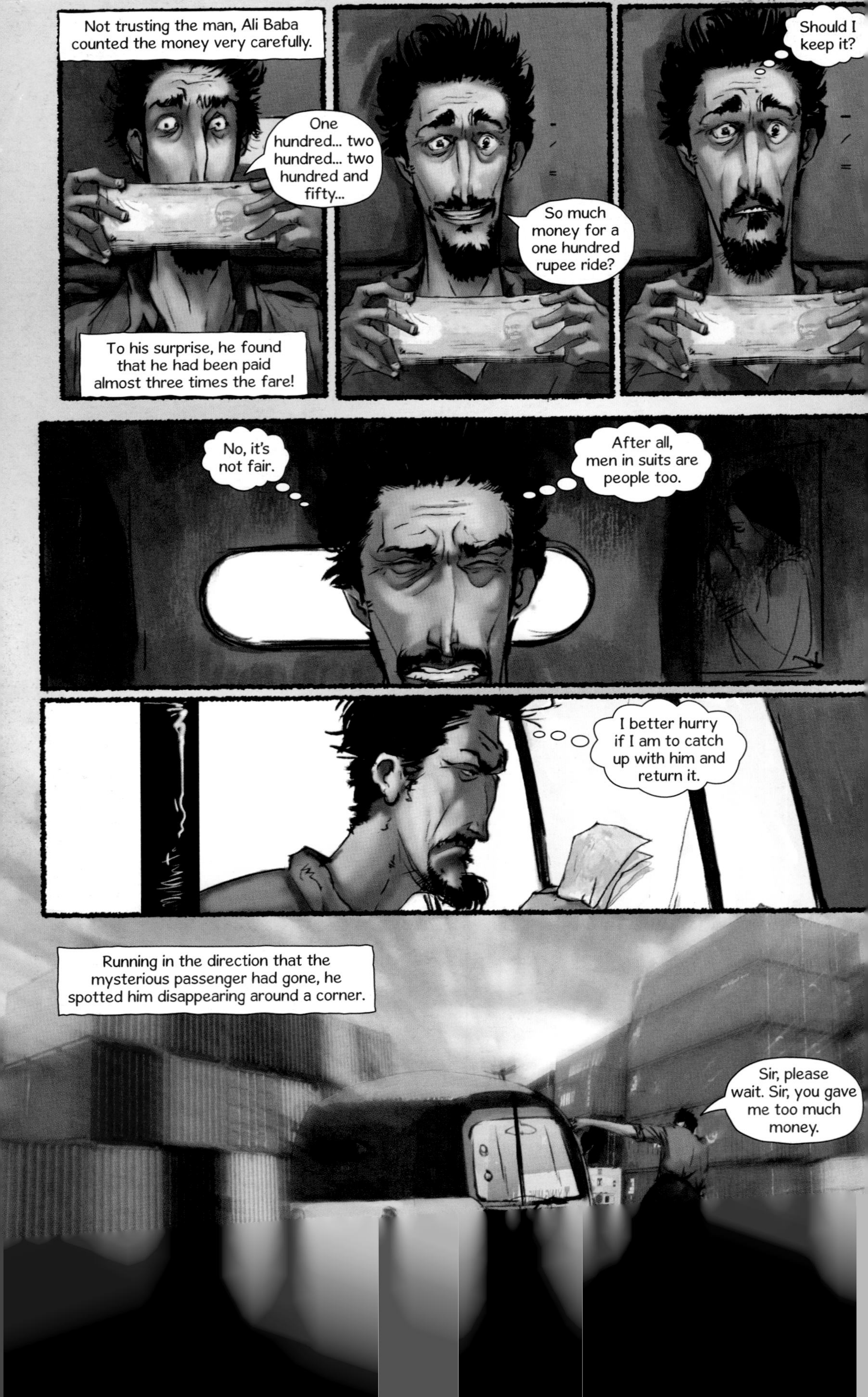
Not trusting the man, Ali Baba counted the money very carefully.
One hundred... two hundred... two hundred and fifty...
To his surprise, he found that he had been paid almost three times the fare!
So much money for a one hundred rupee ride?
Should I keep it?
No, it's not fair.
After all, men in suits are people too.
I better hurry if I am to catch up with him and return it.
Running in the direction that the mysterious passenger had gone, he spotted him disappearing around a corner.
Sir, please wait. Sir, you gave me too much money.

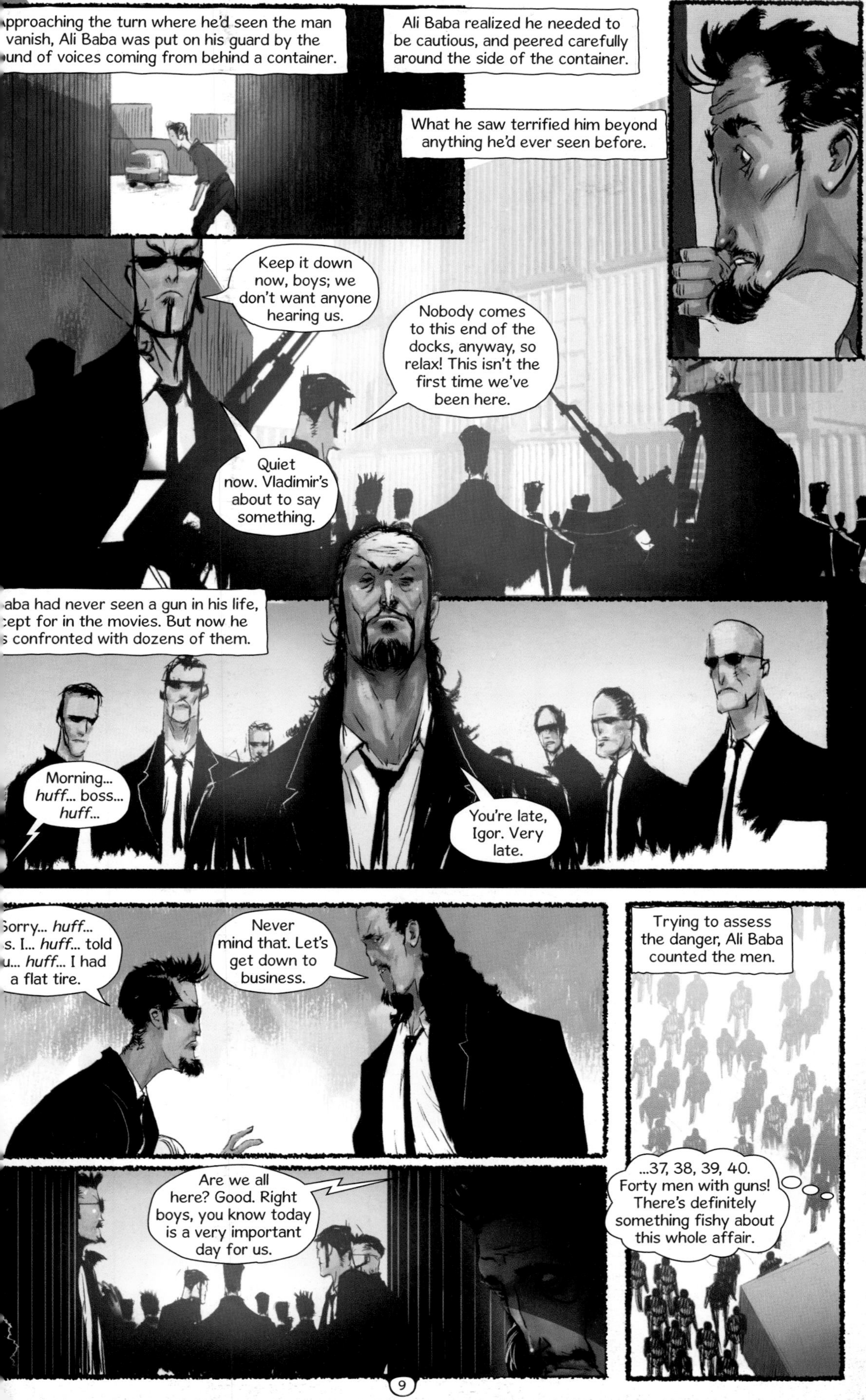
pproaching the turn where he'd seen the man vanish, Ali Baba was put on his guard by the und of voices coming from behind a container.
Ali Baba realized he needed to be cautious, and peered carefully around the side of the container.
What he saw terrified him beyond anything he'd ever seen before.
Keep it down now, boys; we don't want anyone hearing us.
Nobody comes to this end of the docks, anyway, so relax! This isn't the first time we've been here.
Quiet now. Vladimir's about to say something.
aba had never seen a gun in his life, cept for in the movies. But now he s confronted with dozens of them.
Morning... huff... boss... huff...
You're late, Igor. Very late.
Sorry... huff... s. I... huff... told u... huff... I had a flat tire.
Never mind that. Let's get down to business.
Trying to assess the danger, Ali Baba counted the men.
Are we all here? Good. Right boys, you know today is a very important day for us.
...37, 38, 39, 40. Forty men with guns! There's definitely something fishy about this whole affair.

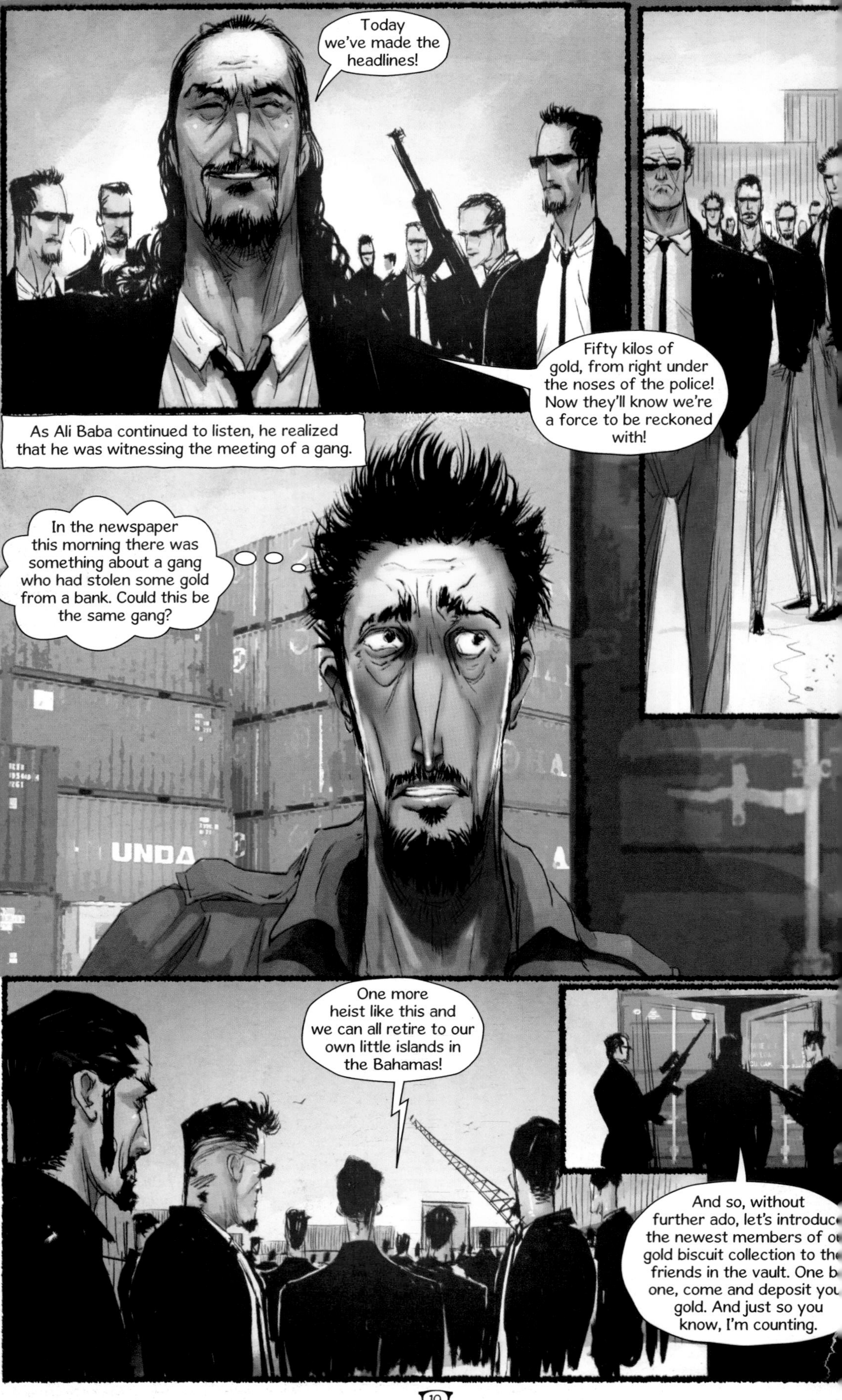
Today we've made the headlines!
Fifty kilos of gold, from right under the noses of the police! Now they'll know we're a force to be reckoned with!
As Ali Baba continued to listen, he realized that he was witnessing the meeting of a gang.
In the newspaper this morning there was something about a gang who had stolen some gold from a bank. Could this be the same gang?
UNDA
One more heist like this and we can all retire to our own little islands in the Bahamas!
And so, without further ado, let's introduc the newest members of o gold biscuit collection to th friends in the vault. One b one, come and deposit you gold. And just so you know, I'm counting.

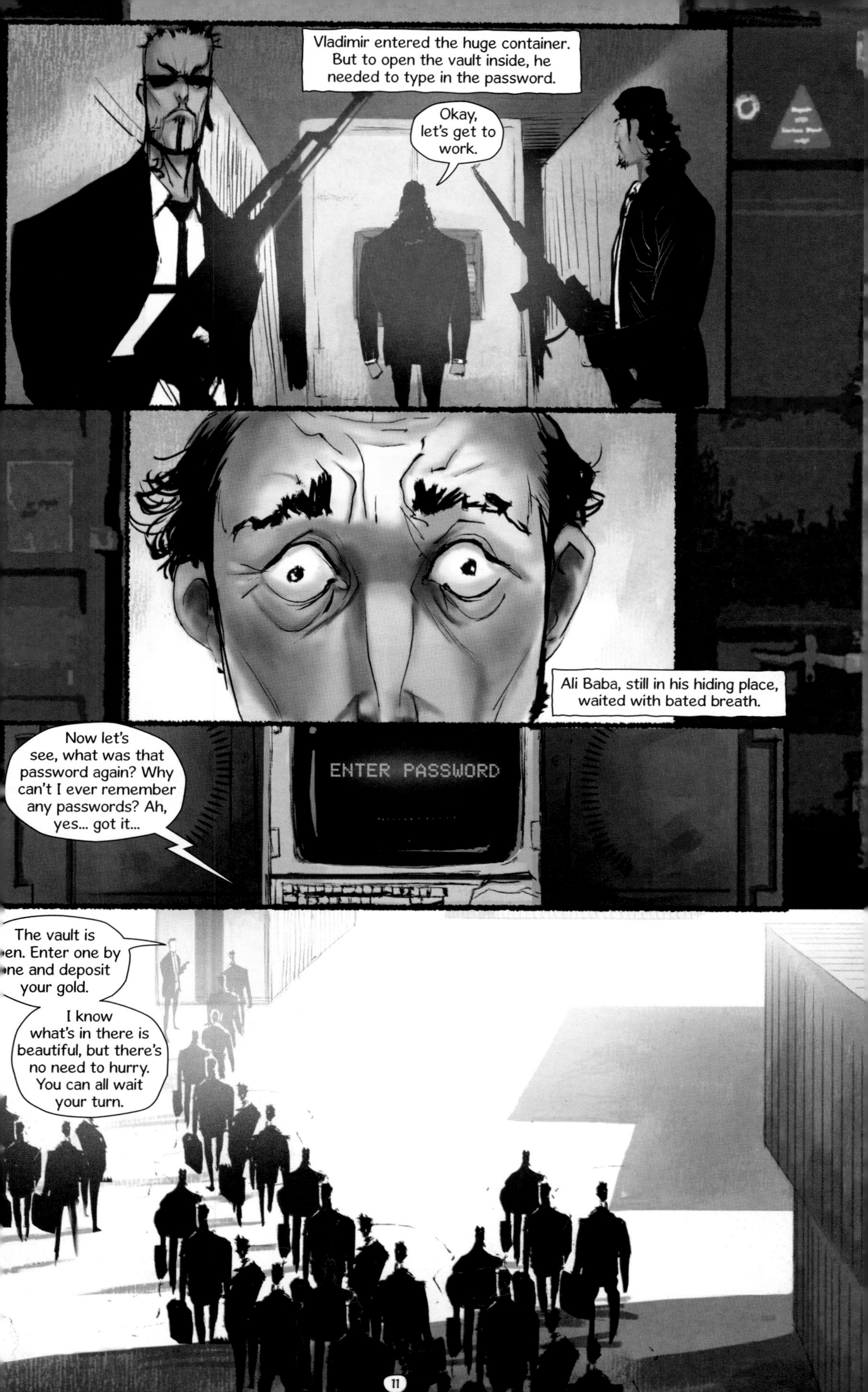

Vladimir entered the huge container. But to open the vault inside, he needed to type in the password.
Okay, let's get to work.
Ali Baba, still in his hiding place, waited with bated breath.
Now let's see, what was that password again? Why can't I ever remember any passwords? Ah, yes... got it...
ENTER PASSWORD
The vault is en. Enter one by ne and deposit your gold.
I know what's in there is beautiful, but there's no need to hurry. You can all wait your turn.

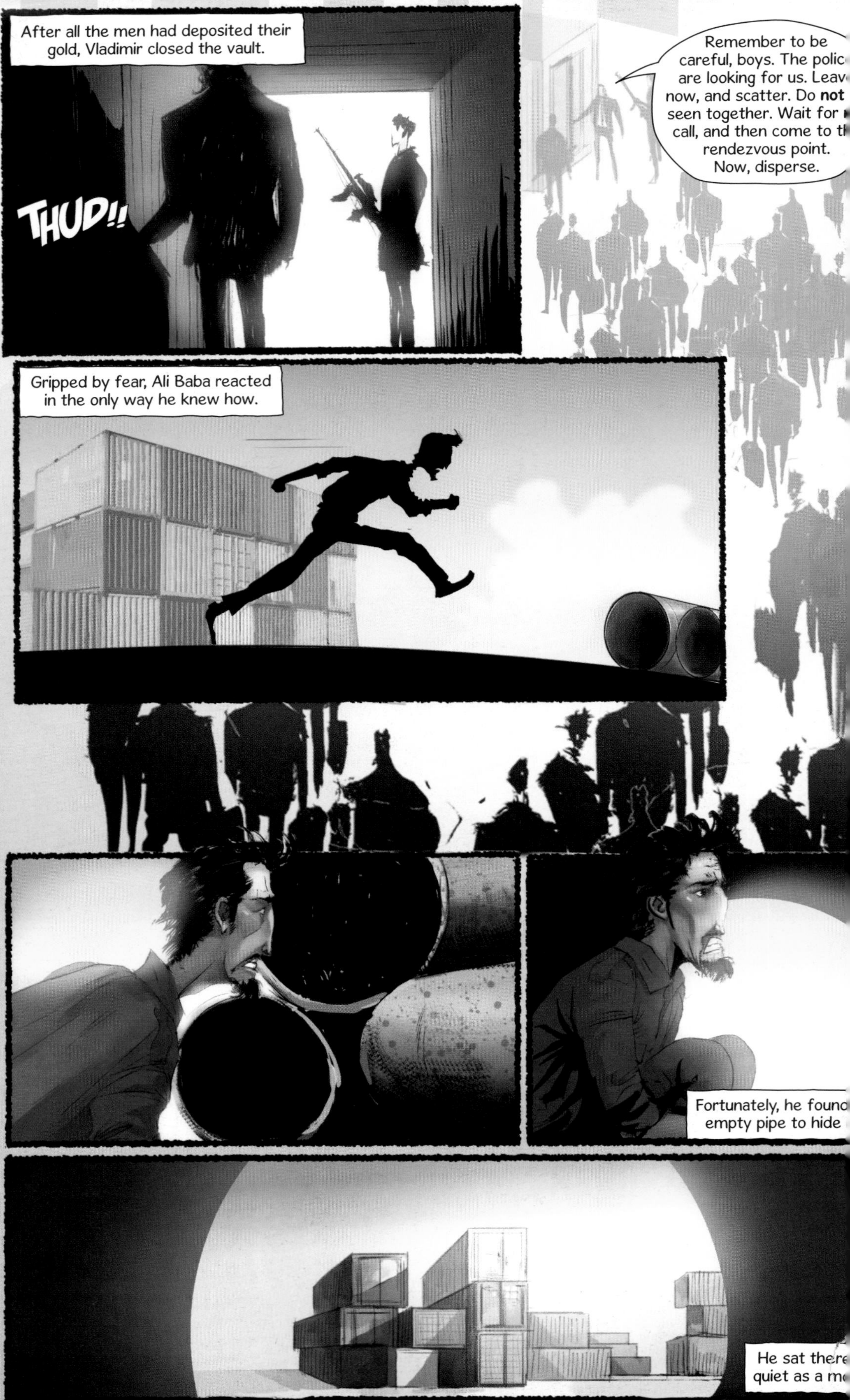
After all the men had deposited their gold, Vladimir closed the vault.
THUD!!
Remember to be careful, boys. The polic are looking for us. Leav now, and scatter. Do not seen together. Wait for call, and then come to t rendezvous point. Now, disperse.
Gripped by fear, Ali Baba reacted in the only way he knew how.
Fortunately, he found empty pipe to hide
He sat there quiet as a m

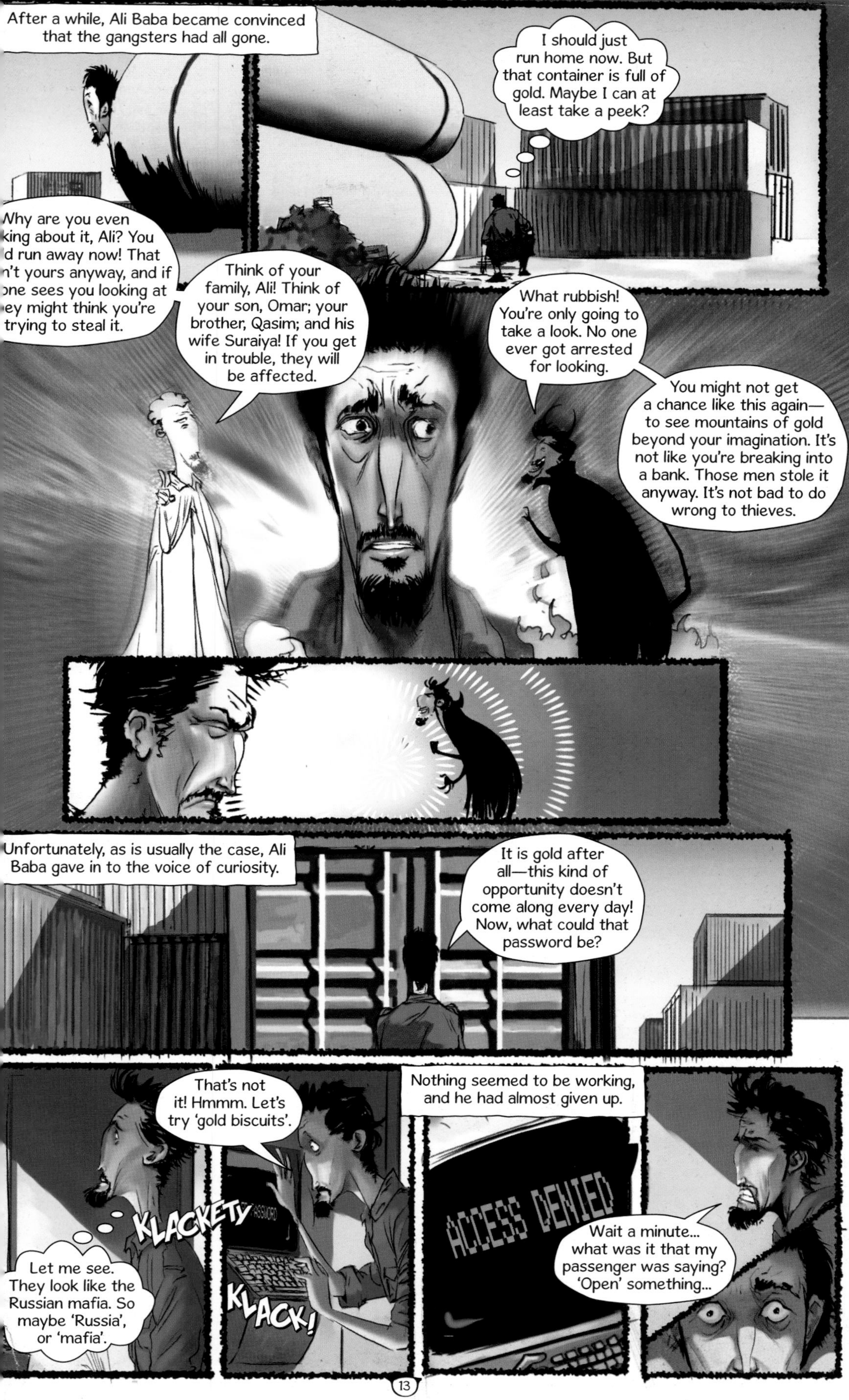

After a while, Ali Baba became convinced that the gangsters had all gone.
I should just run home now. But that container is full of gold. Maybe I can at least take a peek?
Vhy are you even king about it, Ali? You d run away now! That n't yours anyway, and if one sees you looking at ey might think you're trying to steal it.
Think of your family, Ali! Think of your son, Omar; your brother, Qasim; and his wife Suraiya! If you get in trouble, they will be affected.
What rubbish! You're only going to take a look. No one ever got arrested for looking.
You might not get a chance like this again—to see mountains of gold beyond your imagination. It's not like you're breaking into a bank. Those men stole it anyway. It's not bad to do wrong to thieves.
Unfortunately, as is usually the case, Ali Baba gave in to the voice of curiosity.
It is gold after all—this kind of opportunity doesn't come along every day! Now, what could that password be?
Let me see. They look like the Russian mafia. So maybe 'Russia', or 'mafia'.
KLACKETY
That's not it! Hmmm. Let's try 'gold biscuits'.
KLACK!
Nothing seemed to be working, and he had almost given up.
ACCESS DENIED
Wait a minute... what was it that my passenger was saying? 'Open' something...

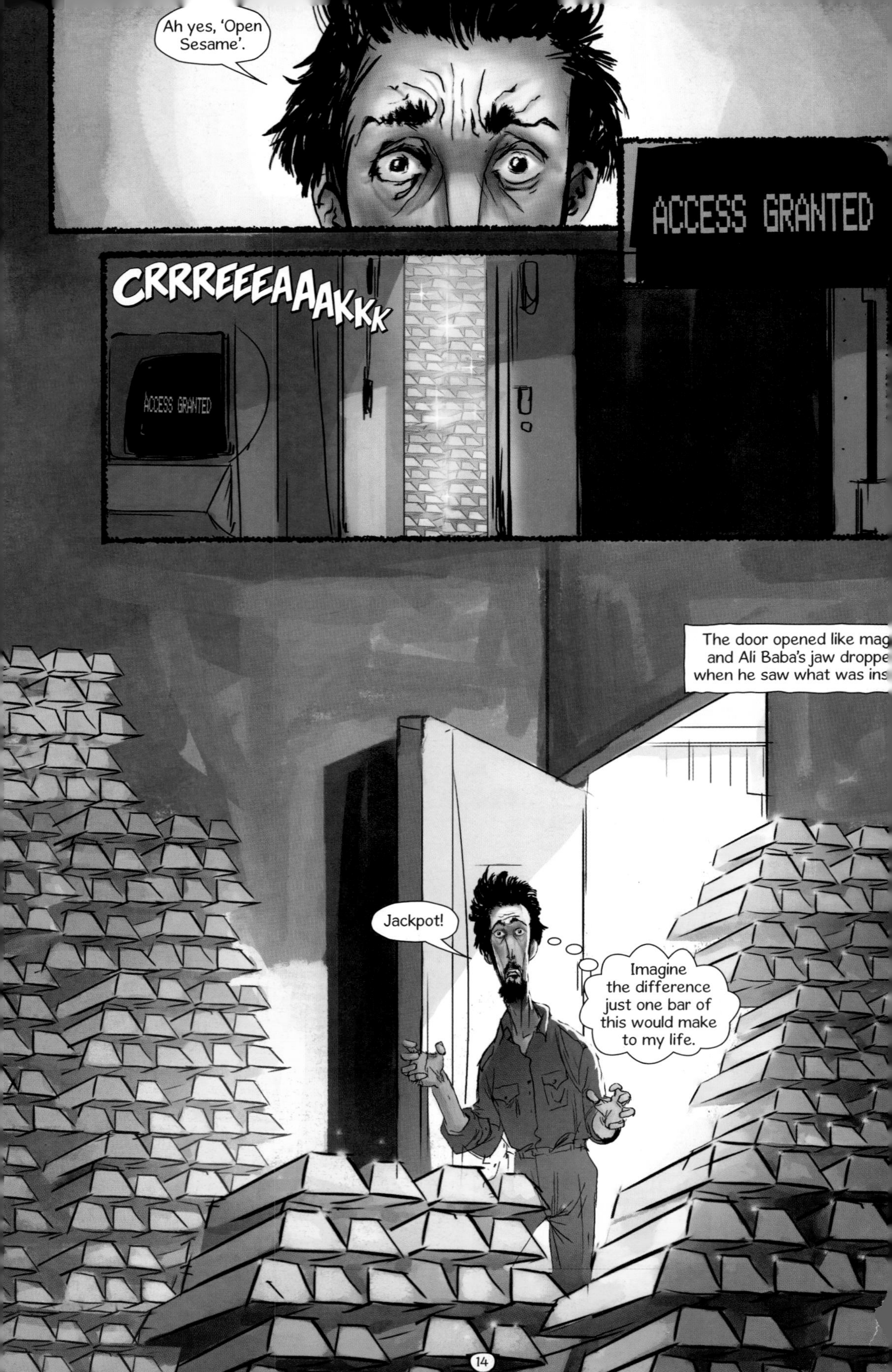

Ah yes, 'Open Sesame'.
ACCESS GRANTED
CRRREEEAAAKKK
ACCESS GRANTED
The door opened like mag
and Ali Baba's jaw droppe
when he saw what was ins
Jackpot!
Imagine the difference just one bar of this would make to my life.

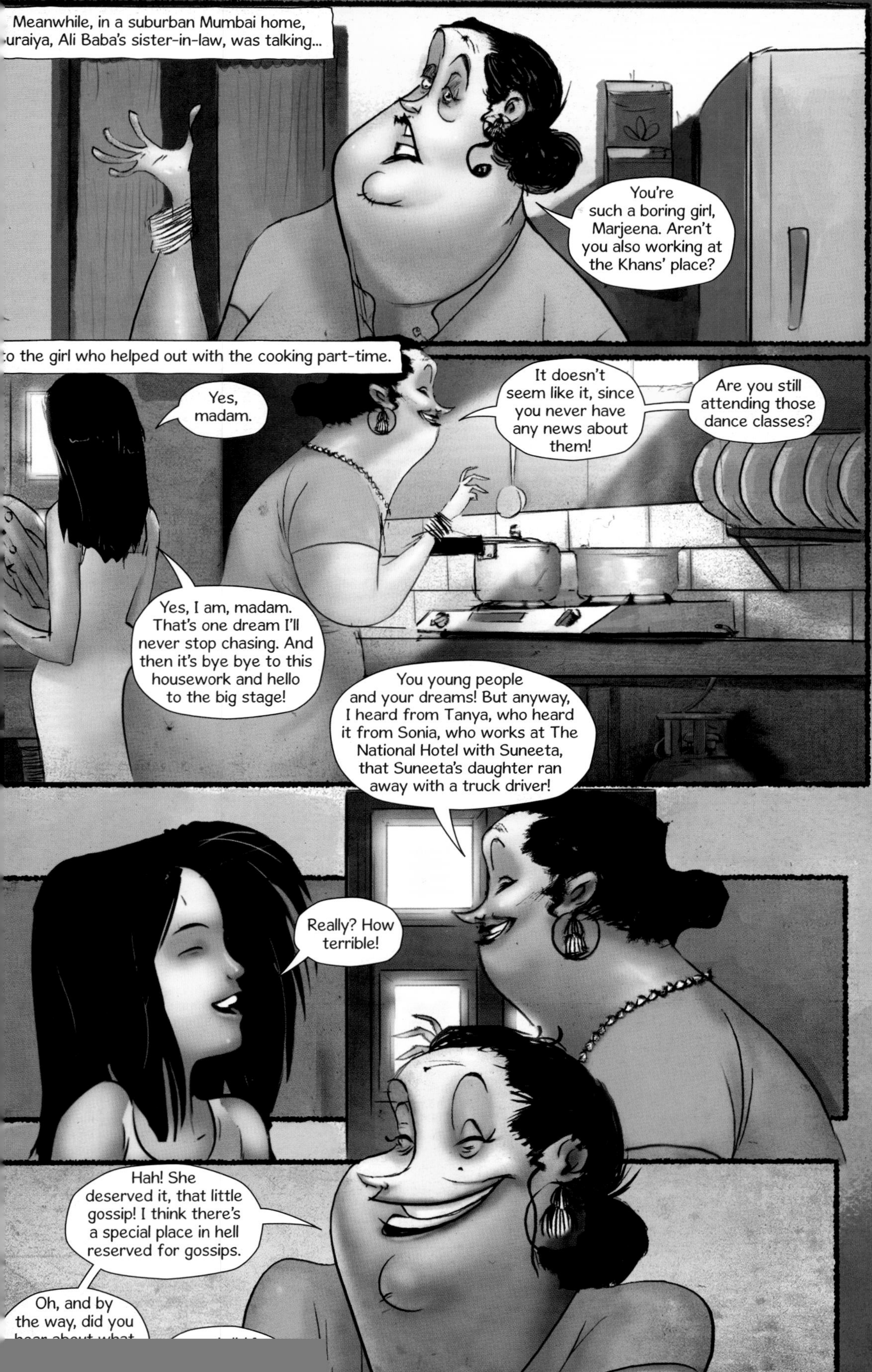

Meanwhile, in a suburban Mumbai home, uraiya, Ali Baba's sister-in-law, was talking...
You're such a boring girl, Marjeena. Aren't you also working at the Khans' place?
o the girl who helped out with the cooking part-time.
Yes, madam.
It doesn't seem like it, since you never have any news about them!
Are you still attending those dance classes?
Yes, I am, madam. That's one dream I'll never stop chasing. And then it's bye bye to this housework and hello to the big stage!
You young people and your dreams! But anyway, I heard from Tanya, who heard it from Sonia, who works at The National Hotel with Suneeta, that Suneeta's daughter ran away with a truck driver!
Really? How terrible!
Hah! She deserved it, that little gossip! I think there's a special place in hell reserved for gossips.
Oh, and by the way, did you

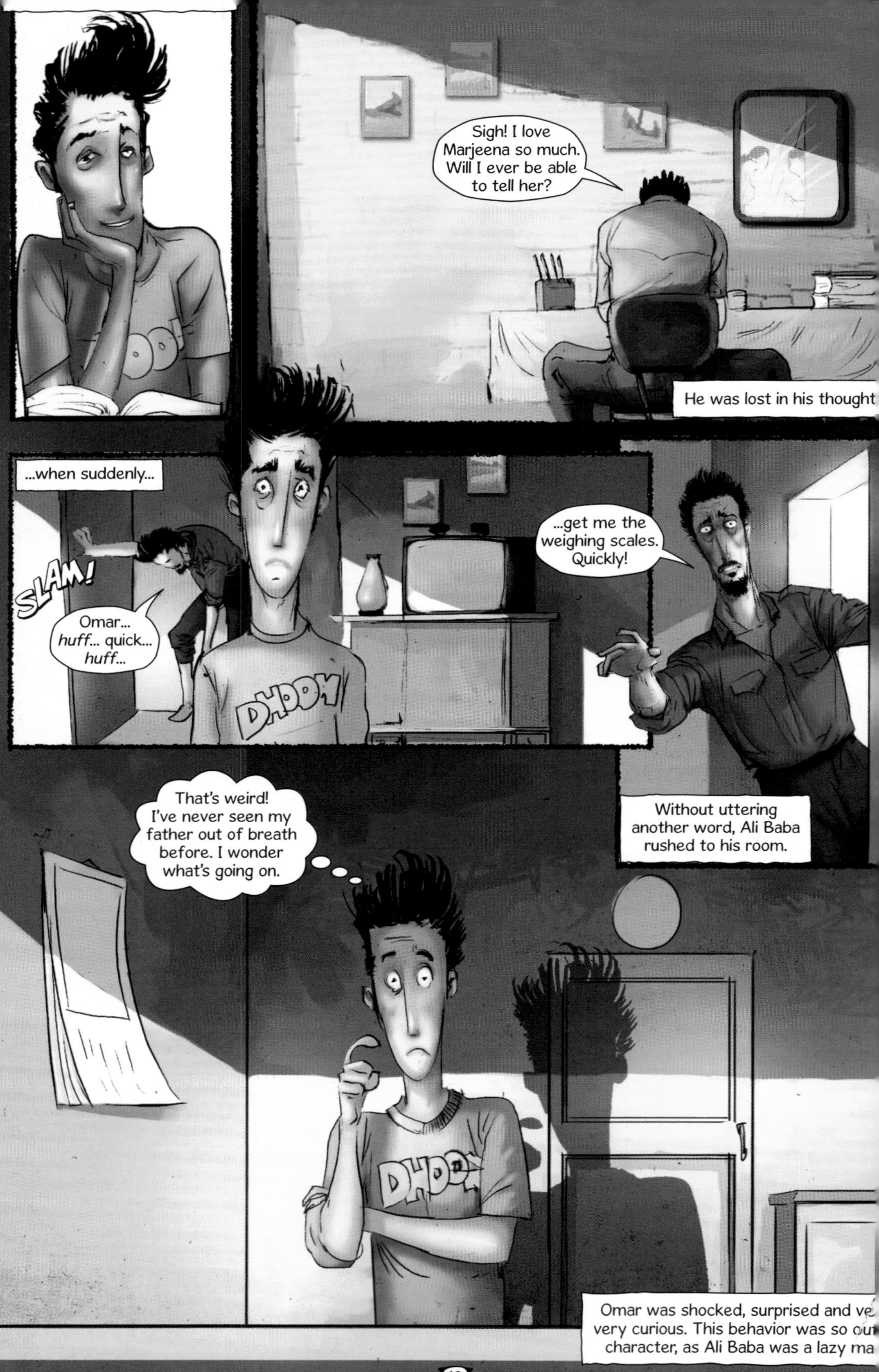
Sigh! I love Marjeena so much. Will I ever be able to tell her?
He was lost in his thought
...when suddenly...
SLAM!
Omar... huff... quick... huff...
...get me the weighing scales. Quickly!
Without uttering another word, Ali Baba rushed to his room.
That's weird! I've never seen my father out of breath before. I wonder what's going on.
Omar was shocked, surprised and ve
very curious. This behavior was so ou
character, as Ali Baba was a lazy ma

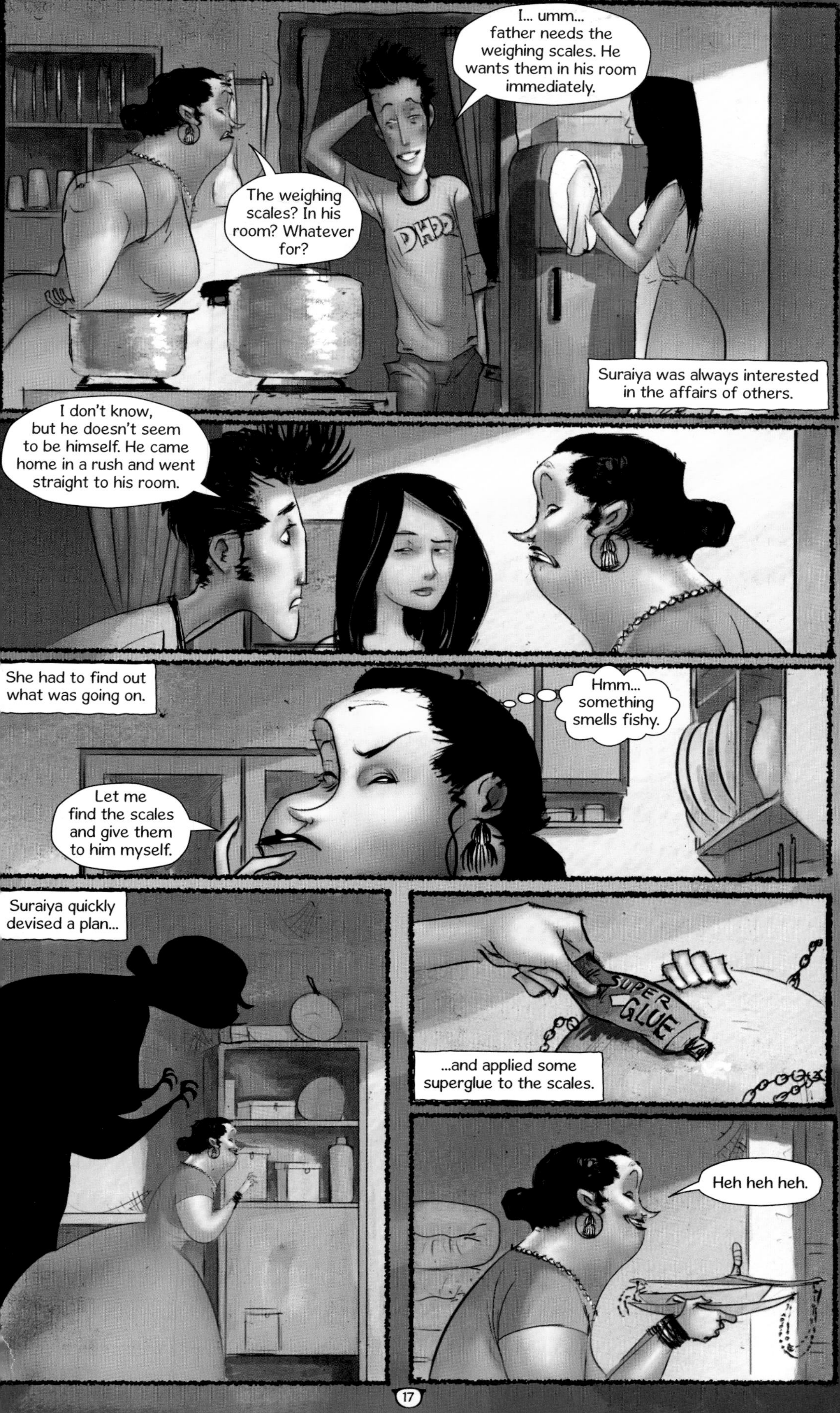
I... umm... father needs the weighing scales. He wants them in his room immediately.
The weighing scales? In his room? Whatever for?
Suraiya was always interested in the affairs of others.
I don't know, but he doesn't seem to be himself. He came home in a rush and went straight to his room.
She had to find out what was going on.
Hmm... something smells fishy.
Let me find the scales and give them to him myself.
Suraiya quickly devised a plan...
SUPER GLUE
...and applied some superglue to the scales.
Heh heh heh.

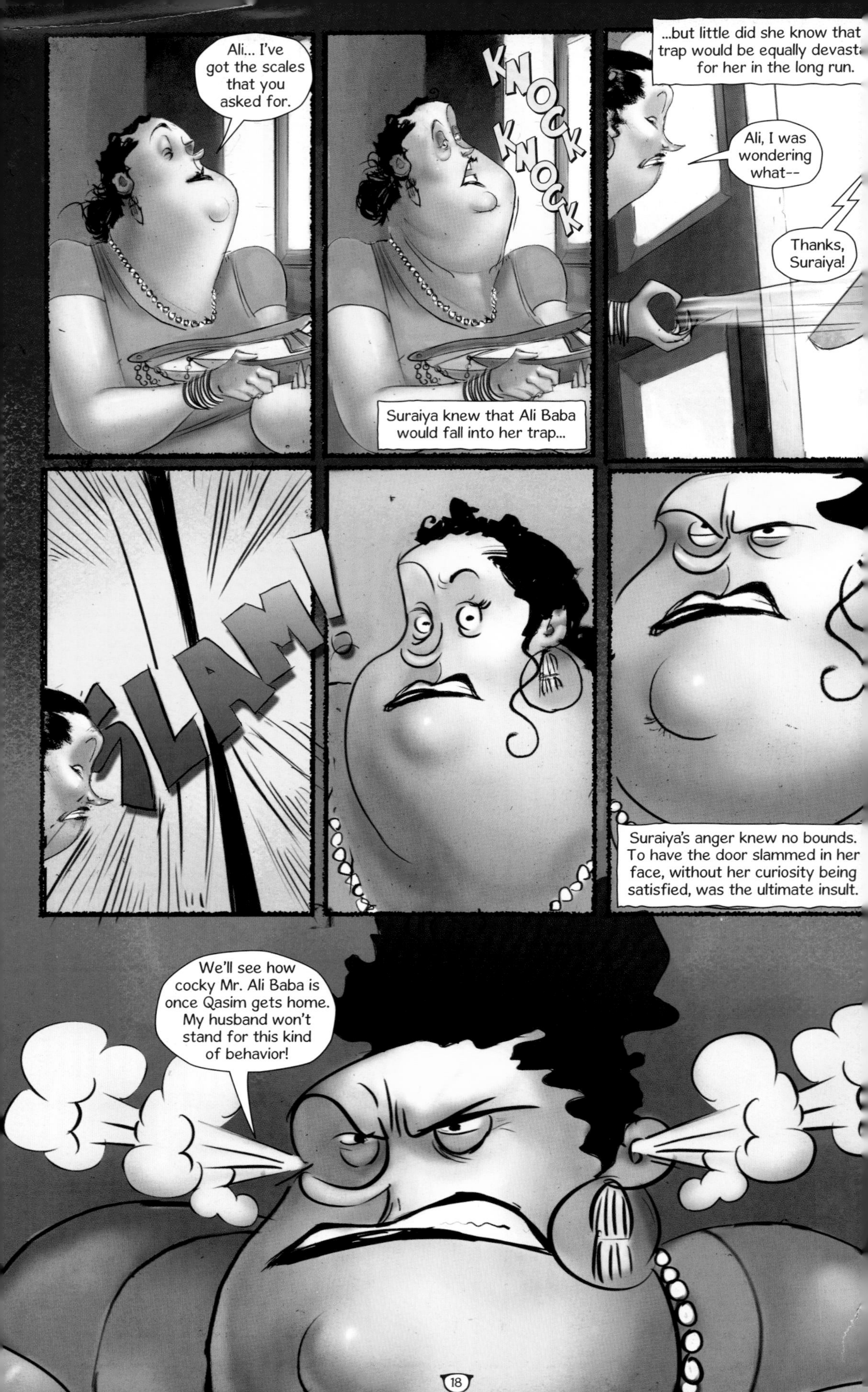

Ali... I've got the scales that you asked for.
KNOCK KNOCK
Suraiya knew that Ali Baba would fall into her trap...
...but little did she know that trap would be equally devast
for her in the long run.
Ali, I was wondering what--
Thanks, Suraiya!
SLAM!
Suraiya's anger knew no bounds. To have the door slammed in her face, without her curiosity being satisfied, was the ultimate insult.
We'll see how cocky Mr. Ali Baba is once Qasim gets home. My husband won't stand for this kind of behavior!

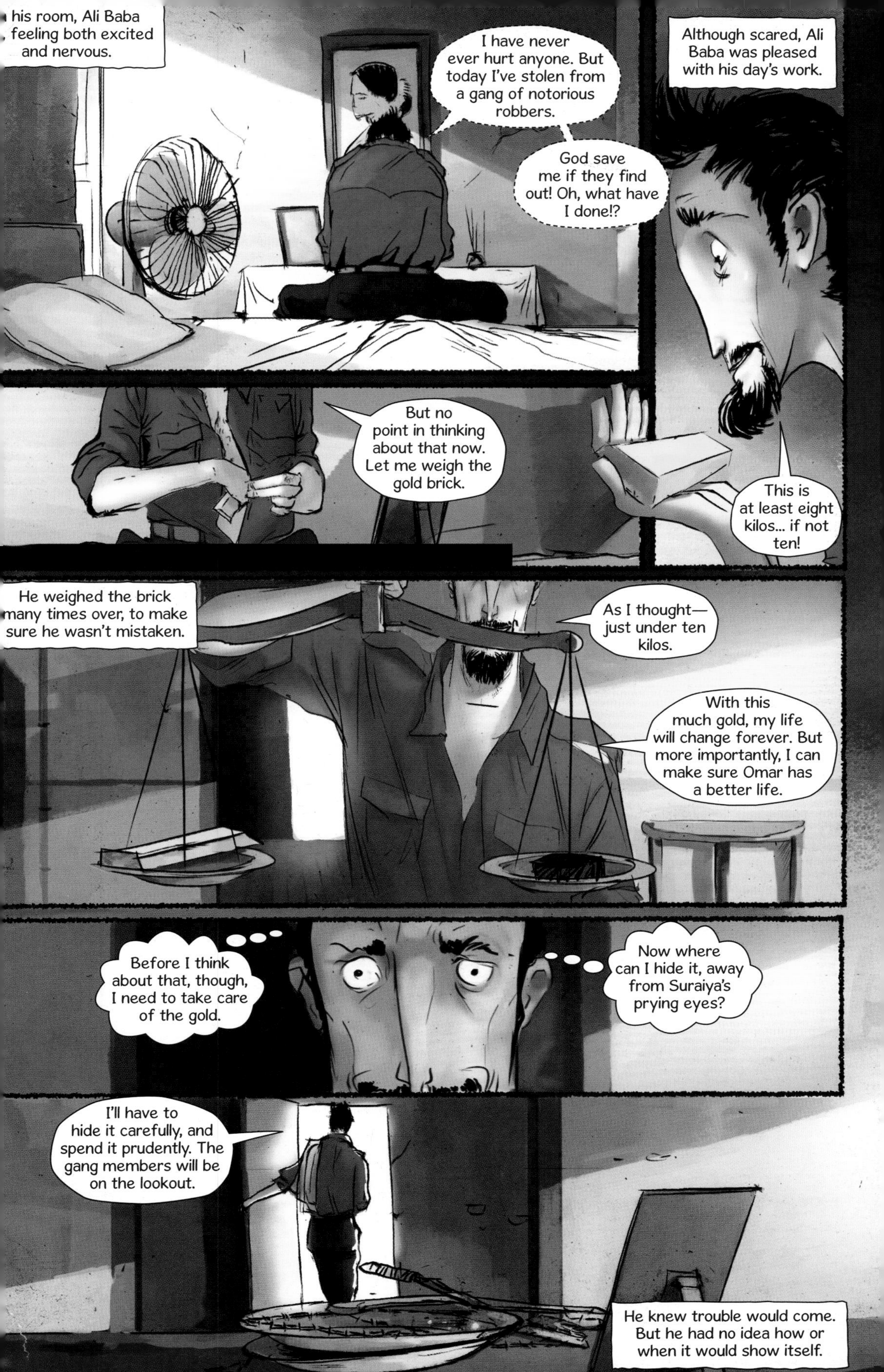

his room, Ali Baba feeling both excited and nervous.
I have never ever hurt anyone. But today I've stolen from a gang of notorious robbers.
God save me if they find out! Oh, what have I done!?
Although scared, Ali Baba was pleased with his day's work.
But no point in thinking about that now. Let me weigh the gold brick.
This is at least eight kilos... if not ten!
He weighed the brick many times over, to make sure he wasn't mistaken.
As I thought—just under ten kilos.
With this much gold, my life will change forever. But more importantly, I can make sure Omar has a better life.
Before I think about that, though, I need to take care of the gold.
Now where can I hide it, away from Suraiya's prying eyes?
I'll have to hide it carefully, and spend it prudently. The gang members will be on the lookout.
He knew trouble would come. But he had no idea how or when it would show itself.

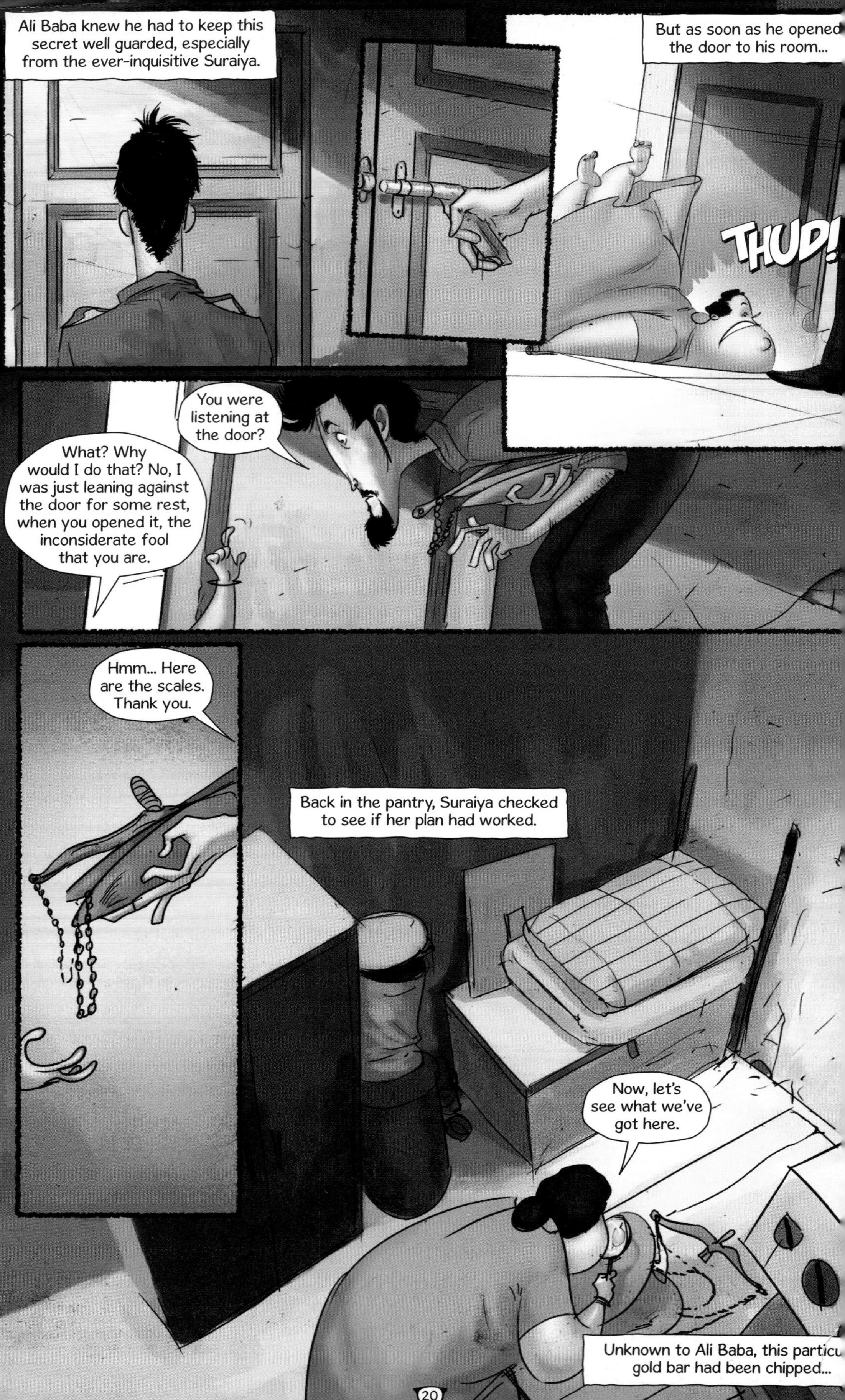
Ali Baba knew he had to keep this secret well guarded, especially from the ever-inquisitive Suraiya.
But as soon as he opened the door to his room...
THUD!
You were listening at the door?
What? Why would I do that? No, I was just leaning against the door for some rest, when you opened it, the inconsiderate fool that you are.
Hmm... Here are the scales. Thank you.
Back in the pantry, Suraiya checked to see if her plan had worked.
Now, let's see what we've got here.
Unknown to Ali Baba, this partic gold bar had been chipped...

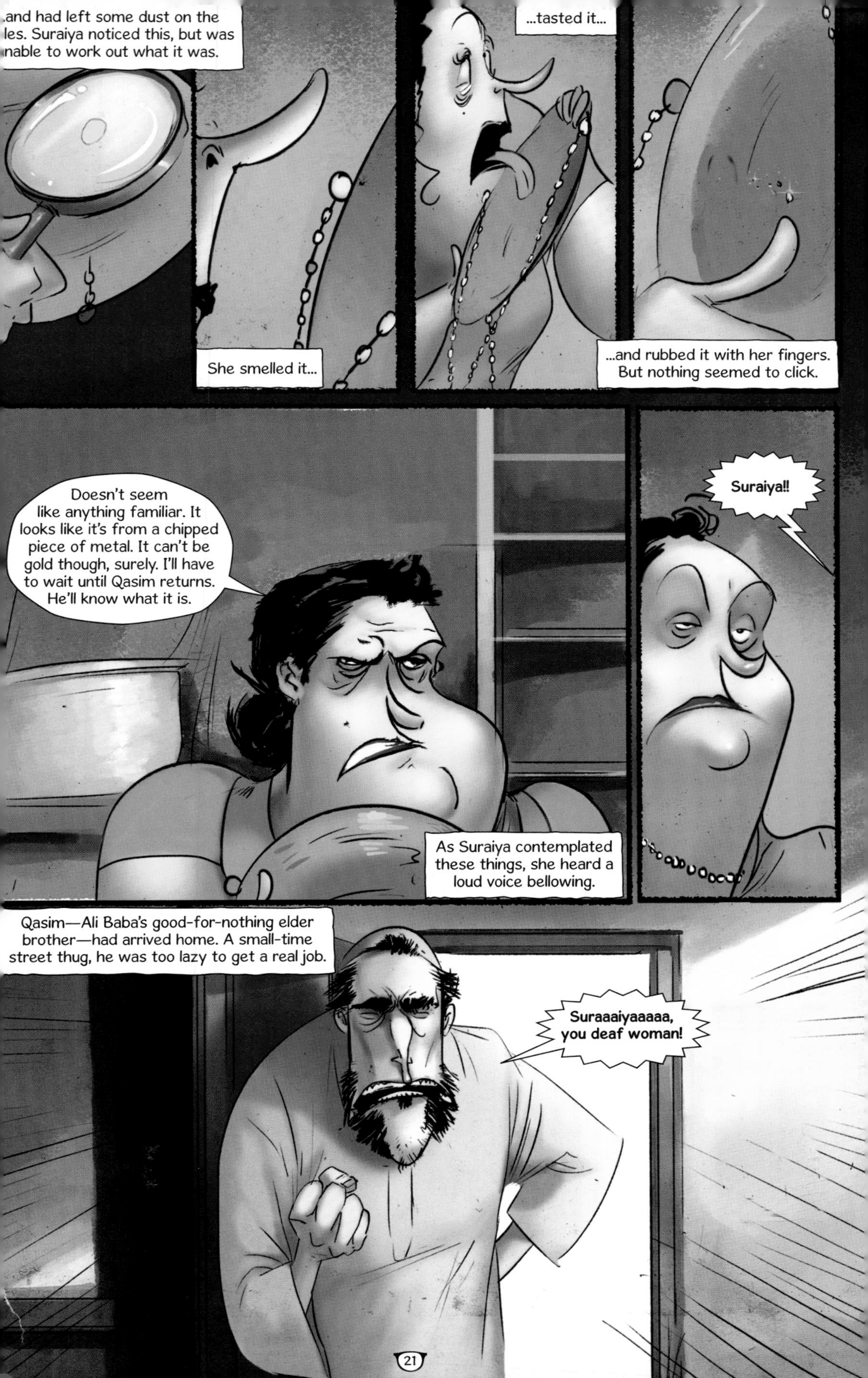

.and had left some dust on the les. Suraiya noticed this, but was nable to work out what it was.
She smelled it...
...tasted it...
...and rubbed it with her fingers. But nothing seemed to click.
Doesn't seem like anything familiar. It looks like it's from a chipped piece of metal. It can't be gold though, surely. I'll have to wait until Qasim returns. He'll know what it is.
As Suraiya contemplated these things, she heard a loud voice bellowing.
Suraiya!!
Qasim—Ali Baba's good-for-nothing elder brother—had arrived home. A small-time street thug, he was too lazy to get a real job.
Suraaaiyaaaaa, you deaf woman!

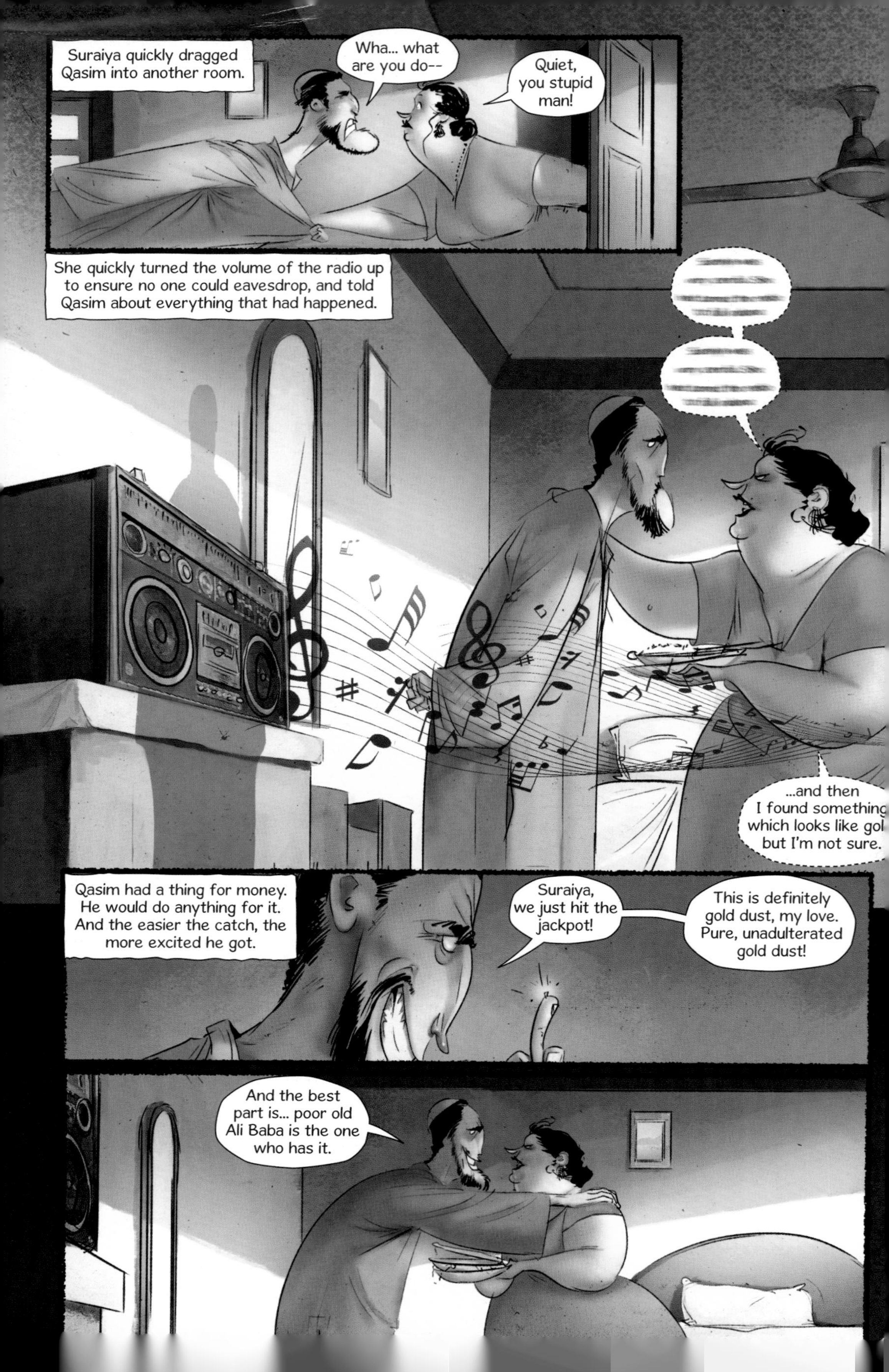
Suraiya quickly dragged Qasim into another room.
Wha... what are you do--
Quiet, you stupid man!
She quickly turned the volume of the radio up to ensure no one could eavesdrop, and told Qasim about everything that had happened.
...and then I found something which looks like gol but I'm not sure.
Qasim had a thing for money. He would do anything for it. And the easier the catch, the more excited he got.
Suraiya, we just hit the jackpot!
This is definitely gold dust, my love. Pure, unadulterated gold dust!
And the best part is... poor old Ali Baba is the one who has it.

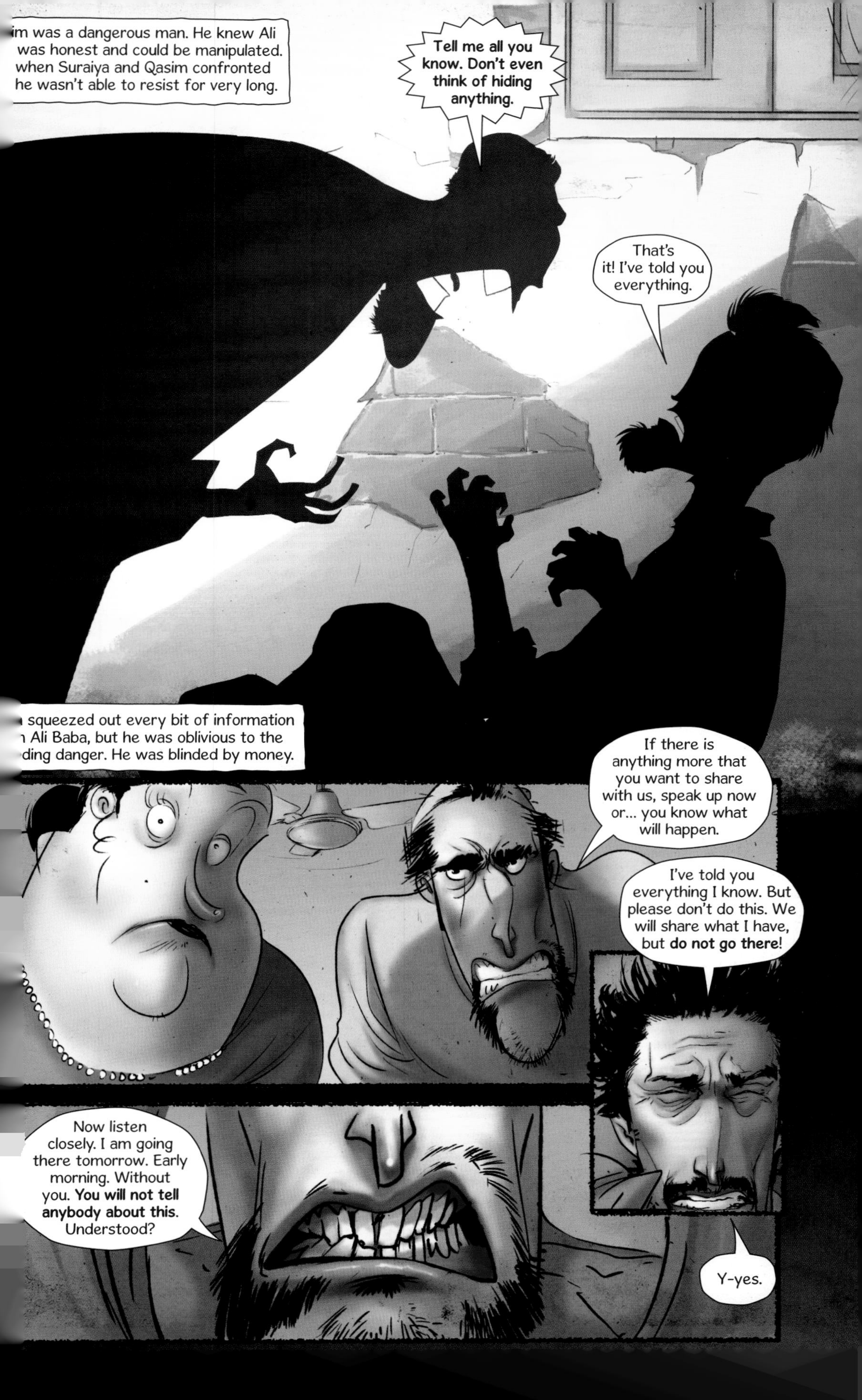
im was a dangerous man. He knew Ali was honest and could be manipulated. when Suraiya and Qasim confronted he wasn't able to resist for very long.
Tell me all you know. Don't even think of hiding anything.
That's it! I've told you everything.
squeezed out every bit of information Ali Baba, but he was oblivious to the ding danger. He was blinded by money.
If there is anything more that you want to share with us, speak up now or... you know what will happen.
I've told you everything I know. But please don't do this. We will share what I have, but **do not go there**!
Now listen closely. I am going there tomorrow. Early morning. Without you. **You will not tell anybody about this.** Understood?
Y-yes.

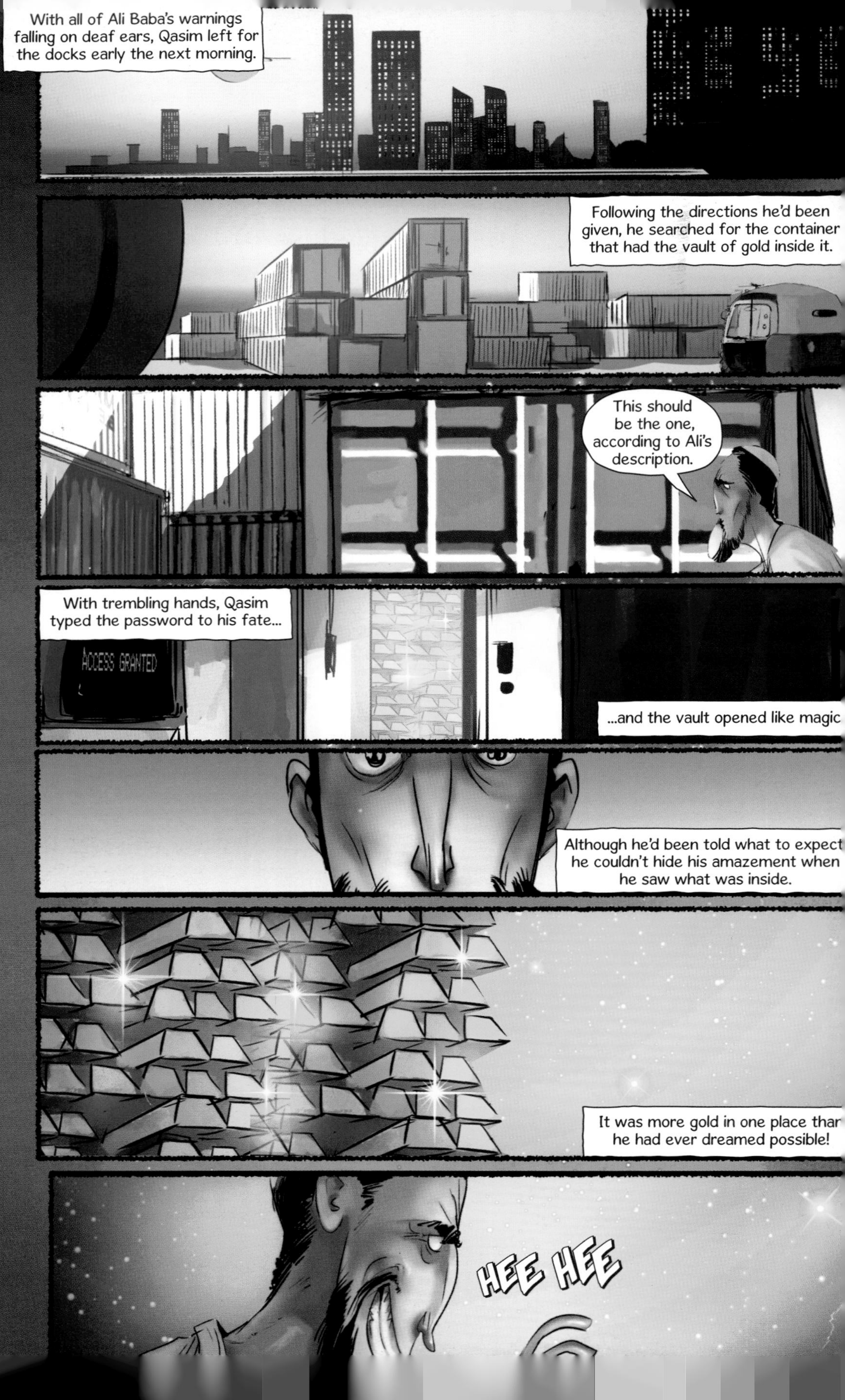
With all of Ali Baba's warnings falling on deaf ears, Qasim left for the docks early the next morning.
Following the directions he'd been given, he searched for the container that had the vault of gold inside it.
This should be the one, according to Ali's description.
With trembling hands, Qasim typed the password to his fate...
ACCESS GRANTED
...and the vault opened like magic
Although he'd been told what to expect he couldn't hide his amazement when he saw what was inside.
It was more gold in one place than he had ever dreamed possible!
HEE HEE

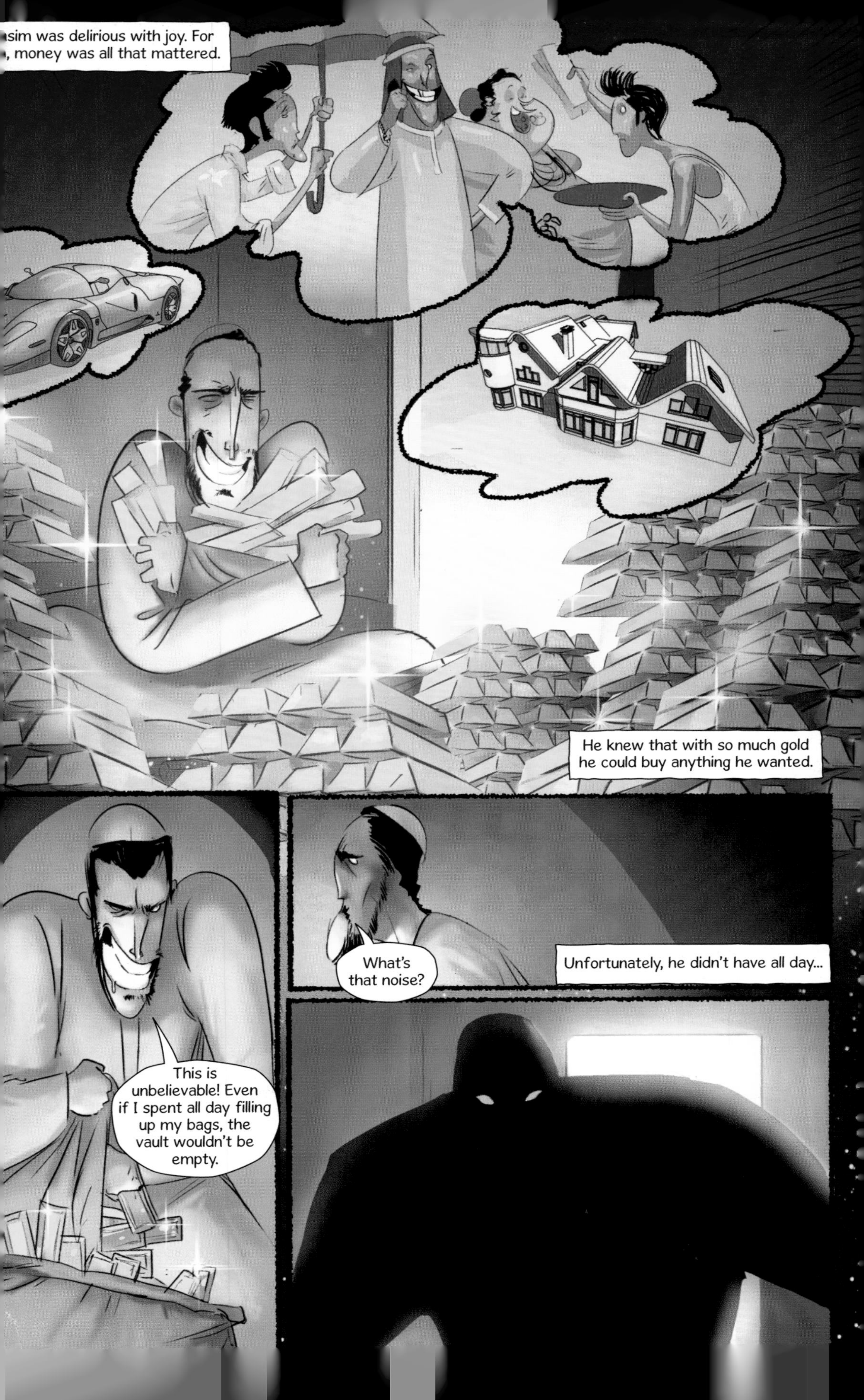
sim was delirious with joy. For
, money was all that mattered.
He knew that with so much gold he could buy anything he wanted.
This is unbelievable! Even if I spent all day filling up my bags, the vault wouldn't be empty.
What's that noise?
Unfortunately, he didn't have all day...

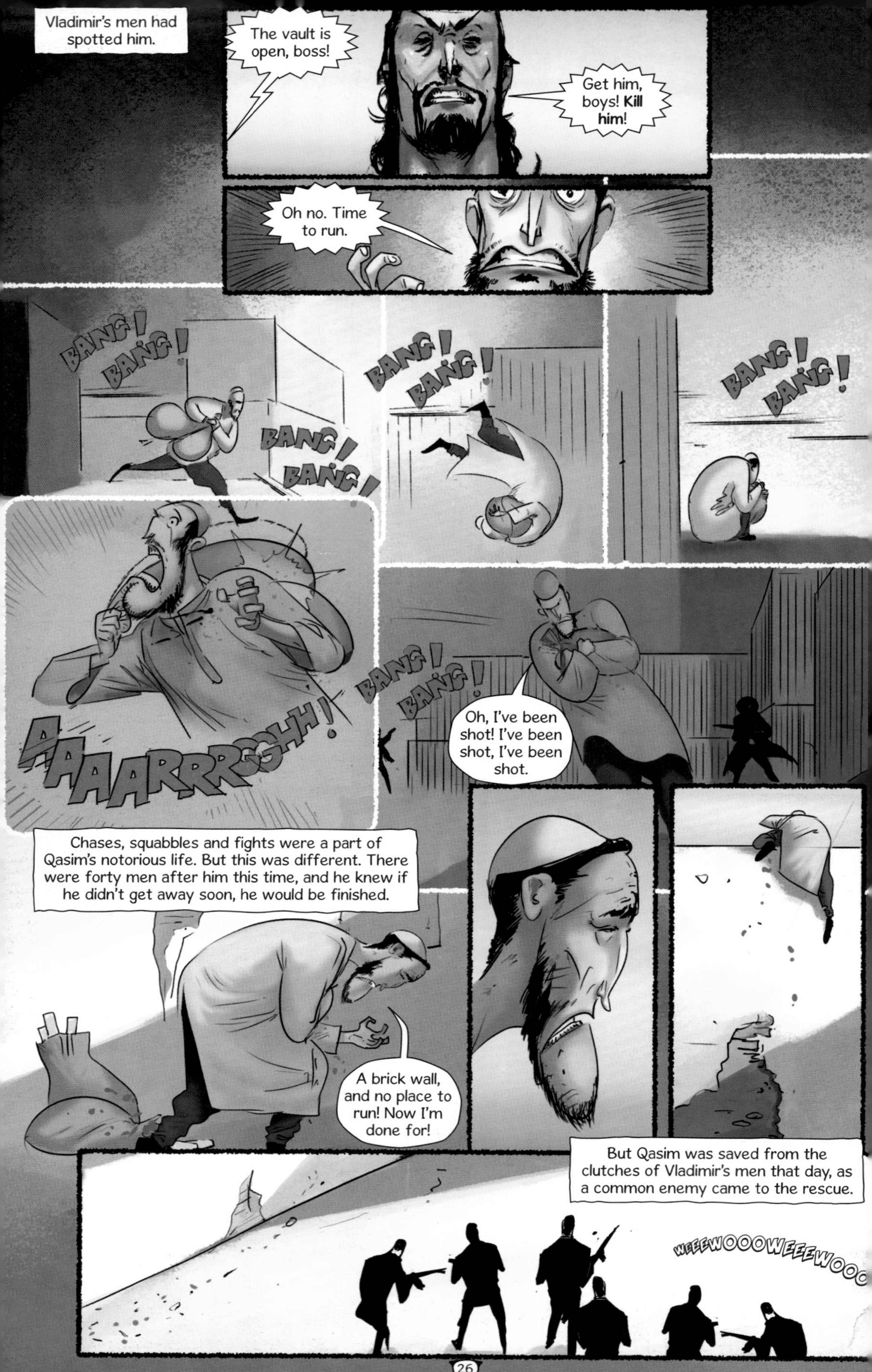

Vladimir's men had spotted him.
The vault is open, boss!
Get him, boys! **Kill him**!
Oh no. Time to run.
BANG! BANG!
BANG! BANG!
BANG! BANG!
BANG! BANG!
AAAARRRGHH!
BANG! BANG!
Oh, I've been shot! I've been shot, I've been shot.
Chases, squabbles and fights were a part of Qasim's notorious life. But this was different. There were forty men after him this time, and he knew if he didn't get away soon, he would be finished.
A brick wall, and no place to run! Now I'm done for!
But Qasim was saved from the clutches of Vladimir's men that day, as a common enemy came to the rescue.
WEEEWOOOWEEEWOOO

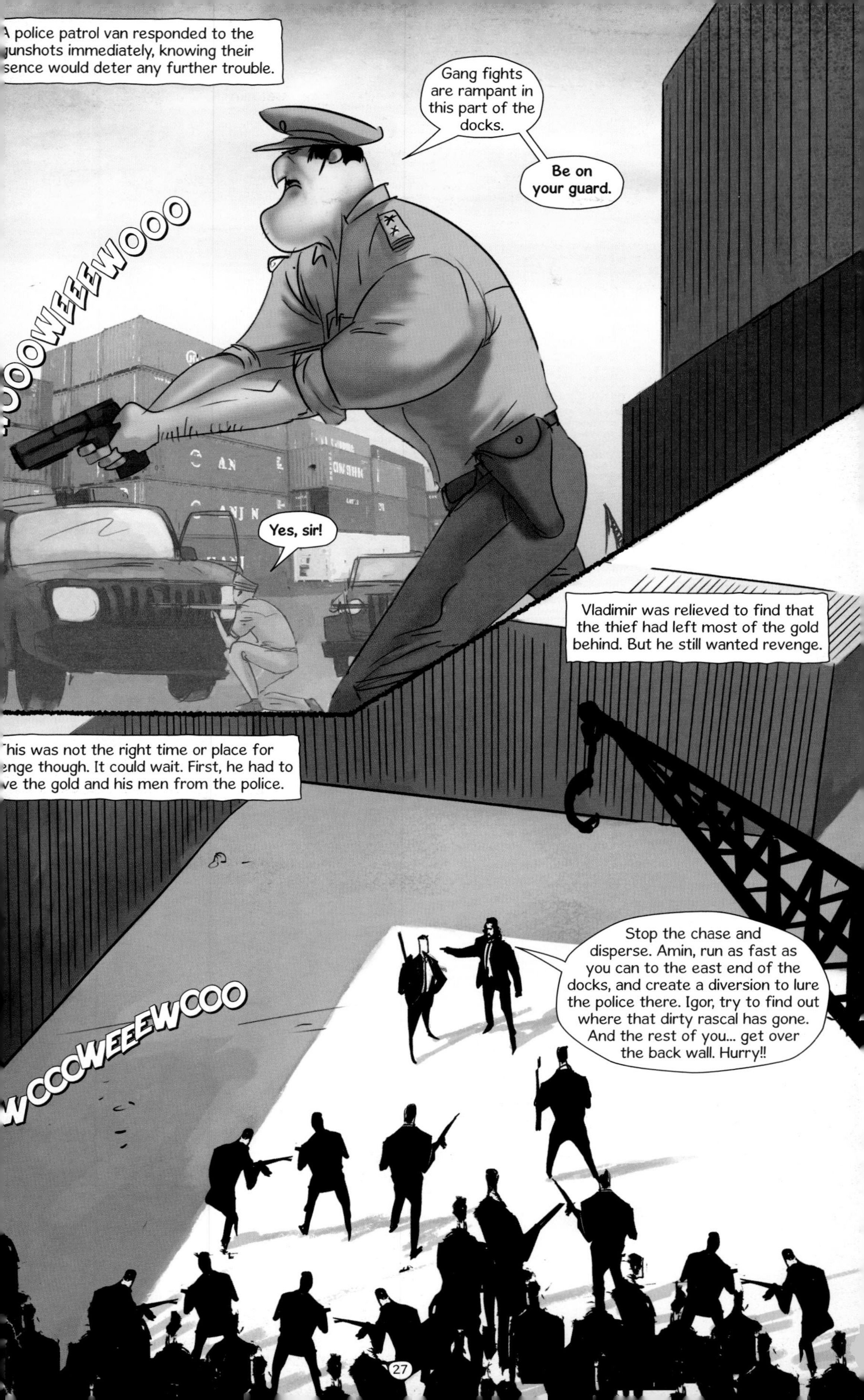
\ police patrol van responded to the
junshots immediately, knowing their
sence would deter any further trouble.
Gang fights are rampant in this part of the docks.
Be on your guard.
OOOWEEEWOOO
Yes, sir!
Vladimir was relieved to find that the thief had left most of the gold behind. But he still wanted revenge.
This was not the right time or place for
enge though. It could wait. First, he had to
ve the gold and his men from the police.
Stop the chase and disperse. Amin, run as fast as you can to the east end of the docks, and create a diversion to lure the police there. Igor, try to find out where that dirty rascal has gone. And the rest of you... get over the back wall. Hurry!!
WCCOWEEEWCOO

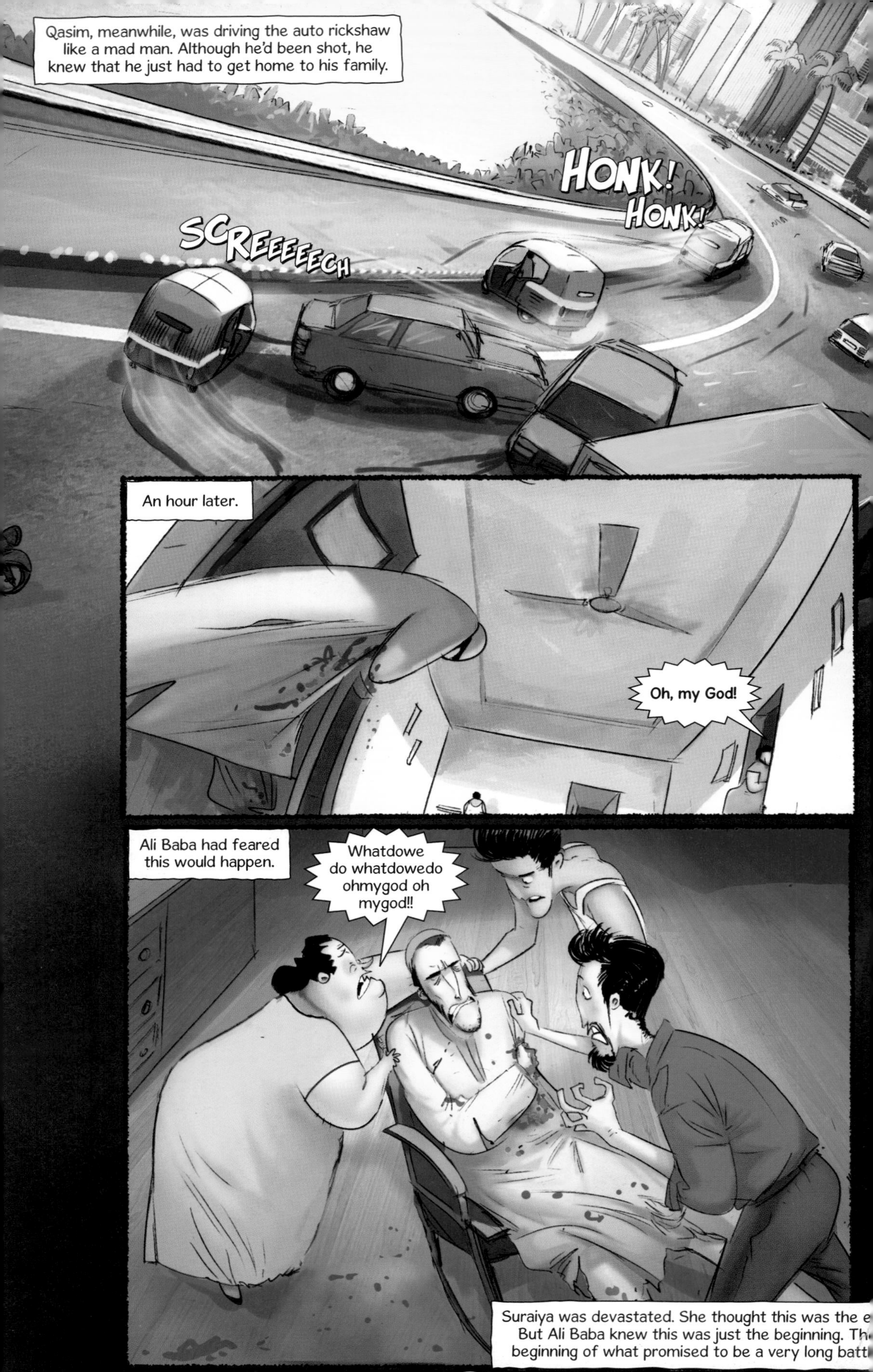
Qasim, meanwhile, was driving the auto rickshaw like a mad man. Although he'd been shot, he knew that he just had to get home to his family.
HONK! HONK!
SCREEEEEECH
An hour later.
Oh, my God!
Ali Baba had feared this would happen.
Whatdowe do whatdowedo ohmygod oh mygod!!
Suraiya was devastated. She thought this was the
But Ali Baba knew this was just the beginning.
beginning of what promised to be a very long

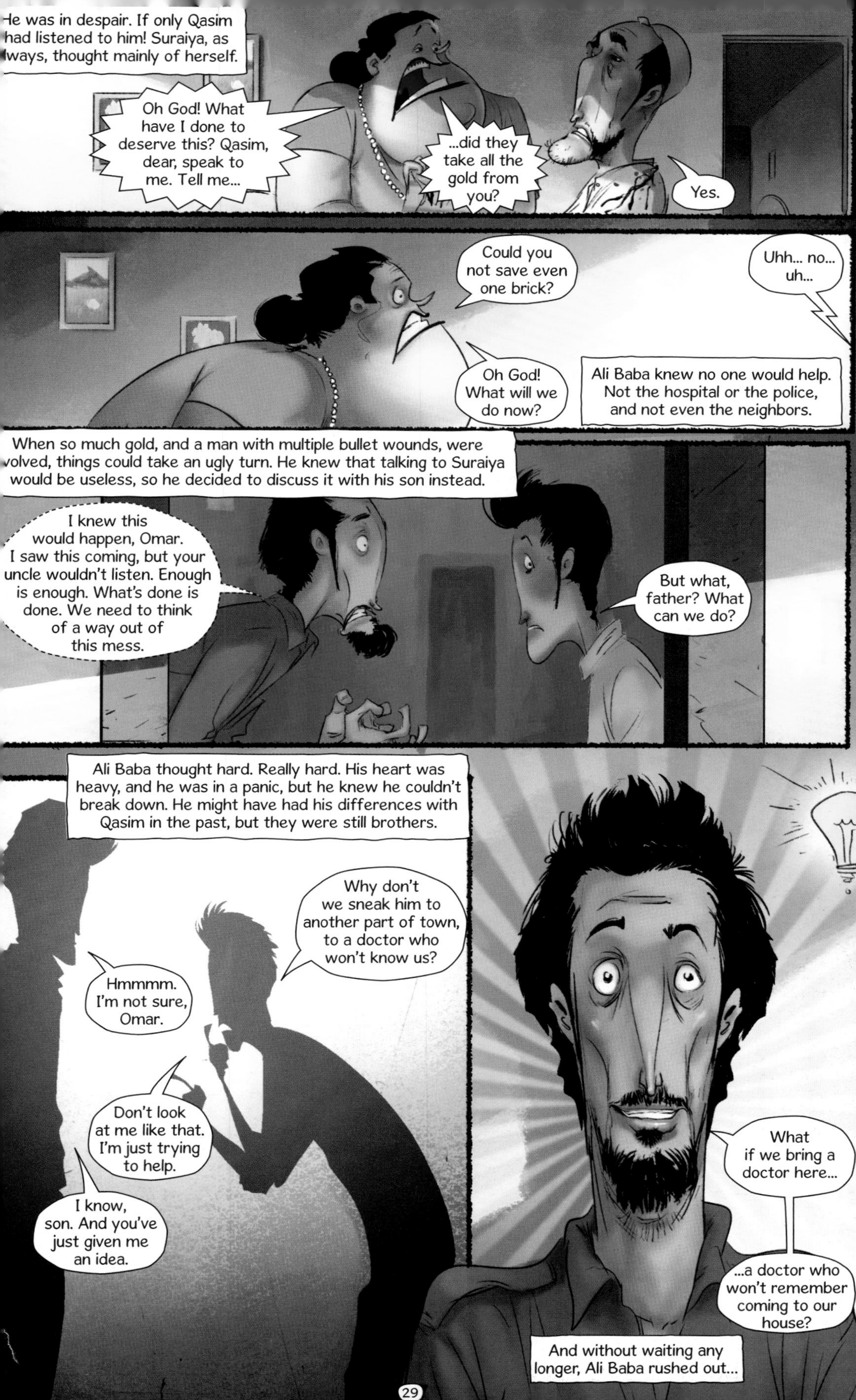
He was in despair. If only Qasim had listened to him! Suraiya, as always, thought mainly of herself.
Oh God! What have I done to deserve this? Qasim, dear, speak to me. Tell me...
...did they take all the gold from you?
Yes.
Could you not save even one brick?
Uhh... no... uh...
Oh God! What will we do now?
Ali Baba knew no one would help. Not the hospital or the police, and not even the neighbors.
When so much gold, and a man with multiple bullet wounds, were involved, things could take an ugly turn. He knew that talking to Suraiya would be useless, so he decided to discuss it with his son instead.
I knew this would happen, Omar. I saw this coming, but your uncle wouldn't listen. Enough is enough. What's done is done. We need to think of a way out of this mess.
But what, father? What can we do?
Ali Baba thought hard. Really hard. His heart was heavy, and he was in a panic, but he knew he couldn't break down. He might have had his differences with Qasim in the past, but they were still brothers.
Why don't we sneak him to another part of town, to a doctor who won't know us?
Hmmmm. I'm not sure, Omar.
Don't look at me like that. I'm just trying to help.
I know, son. And you've just given me an idea.
What if we bring a doctor here...
...a doctor who won't remember coming to our house?
And without waiting any longer, Ali Baba rushed out...

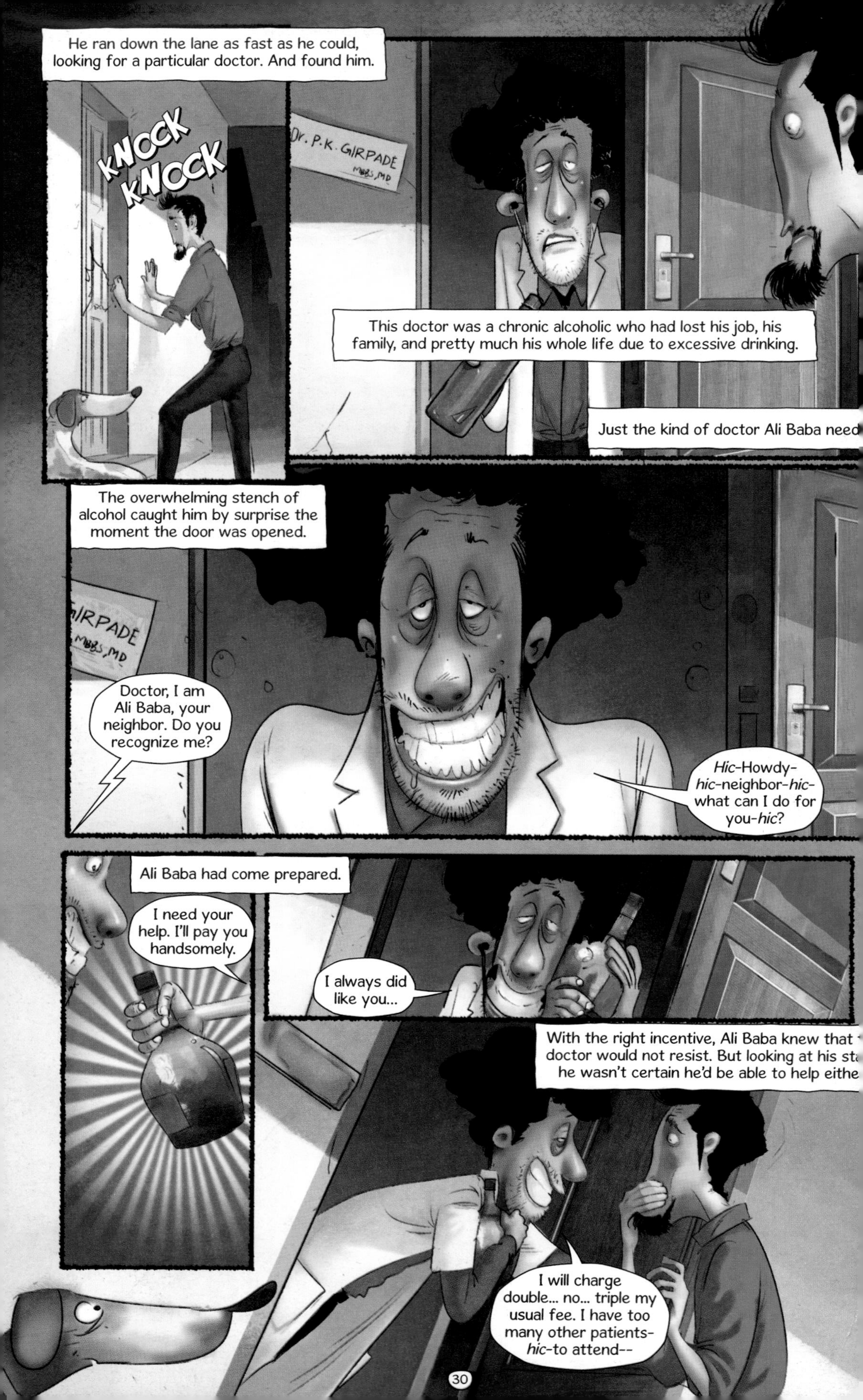
He ran down the lane as fast as he could, looking for a particular doctor. And found him.
KNOCK KNOCK
Dr. P.K. GIRPADE MBBS, MD
This doctor was a chronic alcoholic who had lost his job, his family, and pretty much his whole life due to excessive drinking.
Just the kind of doctor Ali Baba need
The overwhelming stench of alcohol caught him by surprise the moment the door was opened.
GIRPADE MBBS, MD
Doctor, I am Ali Baba, your neighbor. Do you recognize me?
Hic-Howdy-*hic*-neighbor-*hic*-what can I do for you-*hic*?
Ali Baba had come prepared.
I need your help. I'll pay you handsomely.
I always did like you...
With the right incentive, Ali Baba knew that
doctor would not resist. But looking at his st
he wasn't certain he'd be able to help eithe
I will charge double... no... triple my usual fee. I have too many other patients-*hic*-to attend--

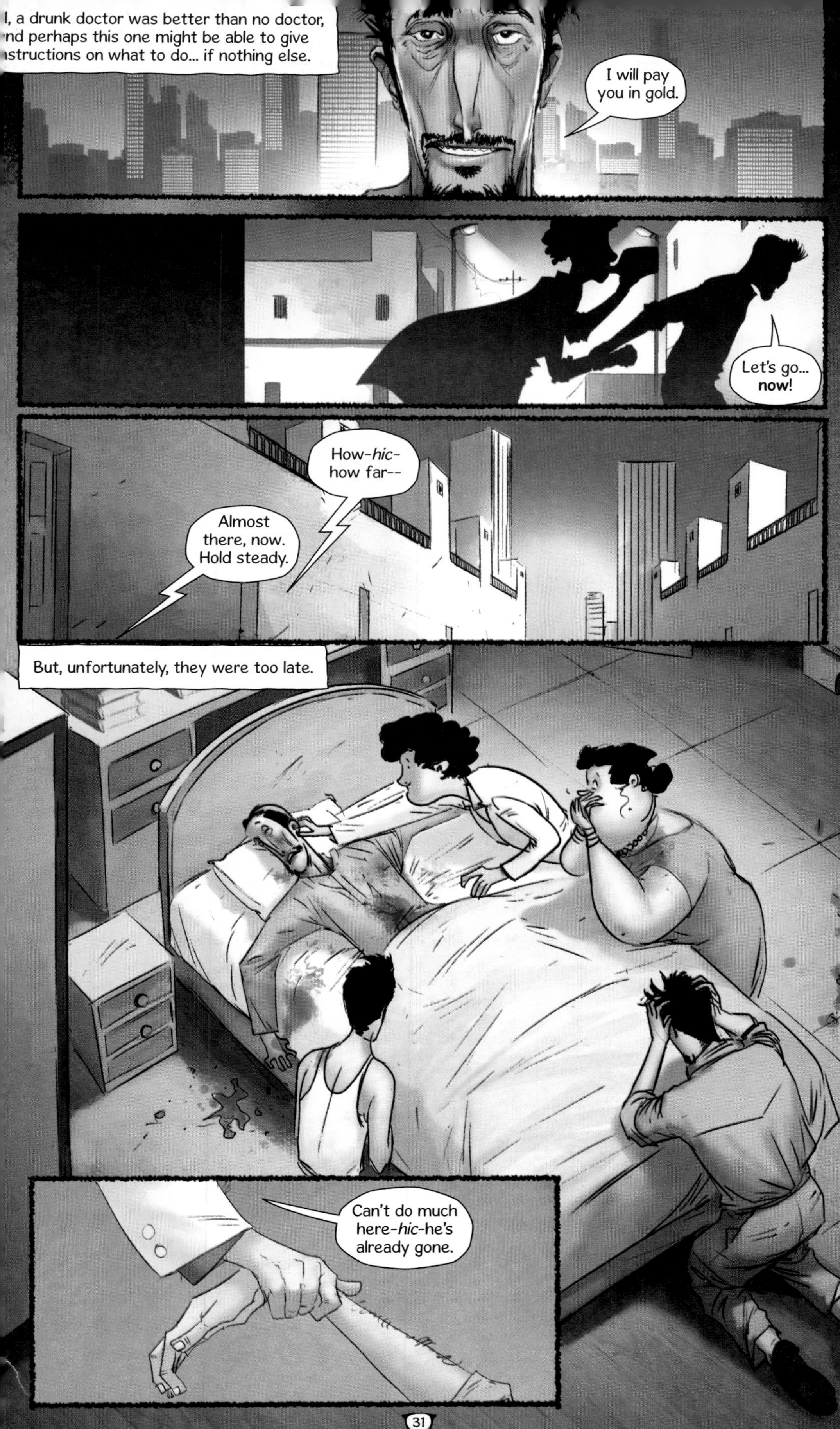
l, a drunk doctor was better than no doctor,
nd perhaps this one might be able to give
nstructions on what to do... if nothing else.
I will pay you in gold.
Let's go... **now!**
How-*hic*-how far--
Almost there, now. Hold steady.
But, unfortunately, they were too late.
Can't do much here-*hic*-he's already gone.

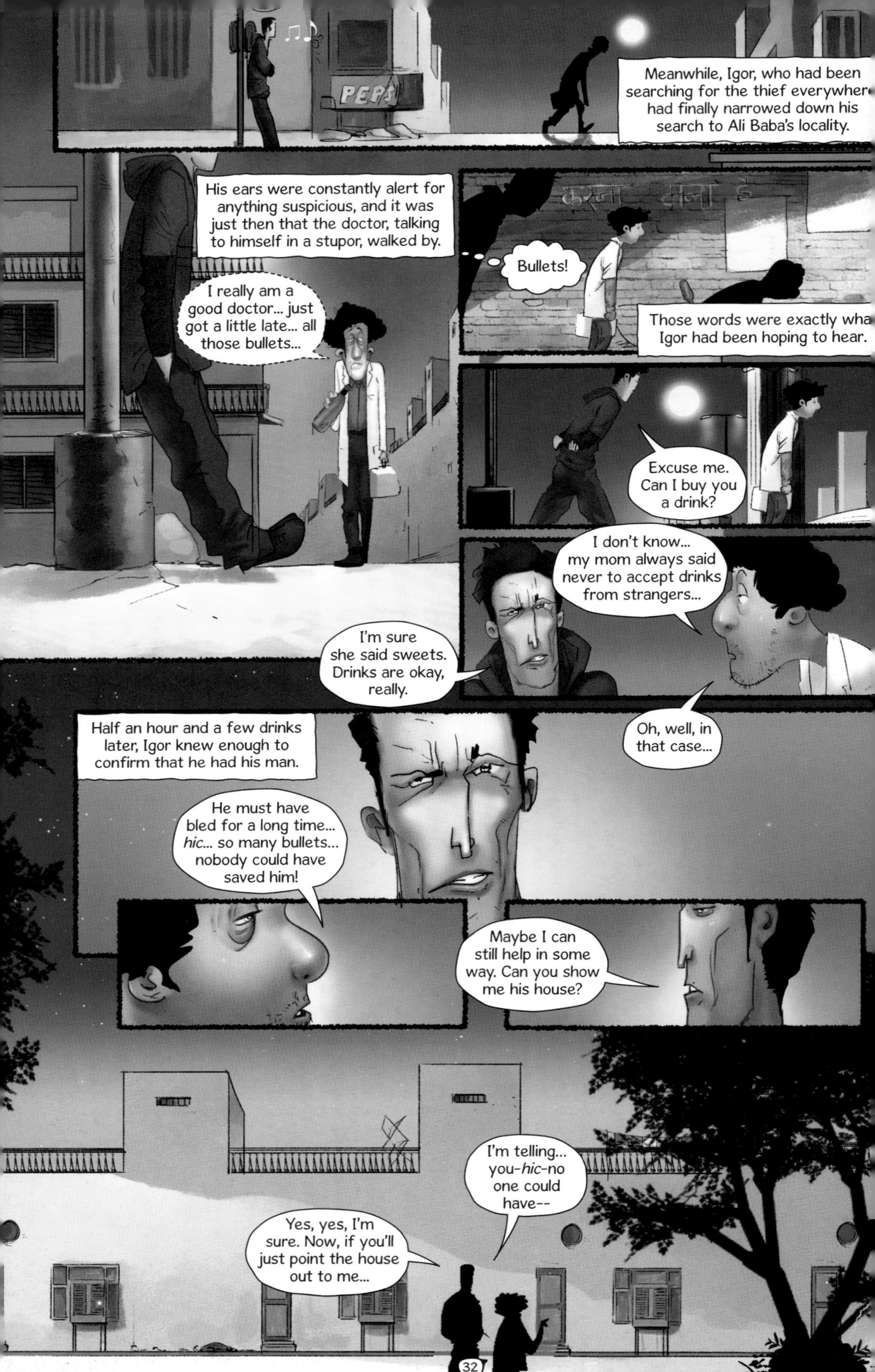
PEPS
Meanwhile, Igor, who had been searching for the thief everywhere had finally narrowed down his search to Ali Baba's locality.
His ears were constantly alert for anything suspicious, and it was just then that the doctor, talking to himself in a stupor, walked by.
I really am a good doctor... just got a little late... all those bullets...
Bullets!
Those words were exactly what Igor had been hoping to hear.
Excuse me. Can I buy you a drink?
I don't know... my mom always said never to accept drinks from strangers...
I'm sure she said sweets. Drinks are okay, really.
Oh, well, in that case...
Half an hour and a few drinks later, Igor knew enough to confirm that he had his man.
He must have bled for a long time... *hic*... so many bullets... nobody could have saved him!
Maybe I can still help in some way. Can you show me his house?
I'm telling... you-*hic*-no one could have--
Yes, yes, I'm sure. Now, if you'll just point the house out to me...

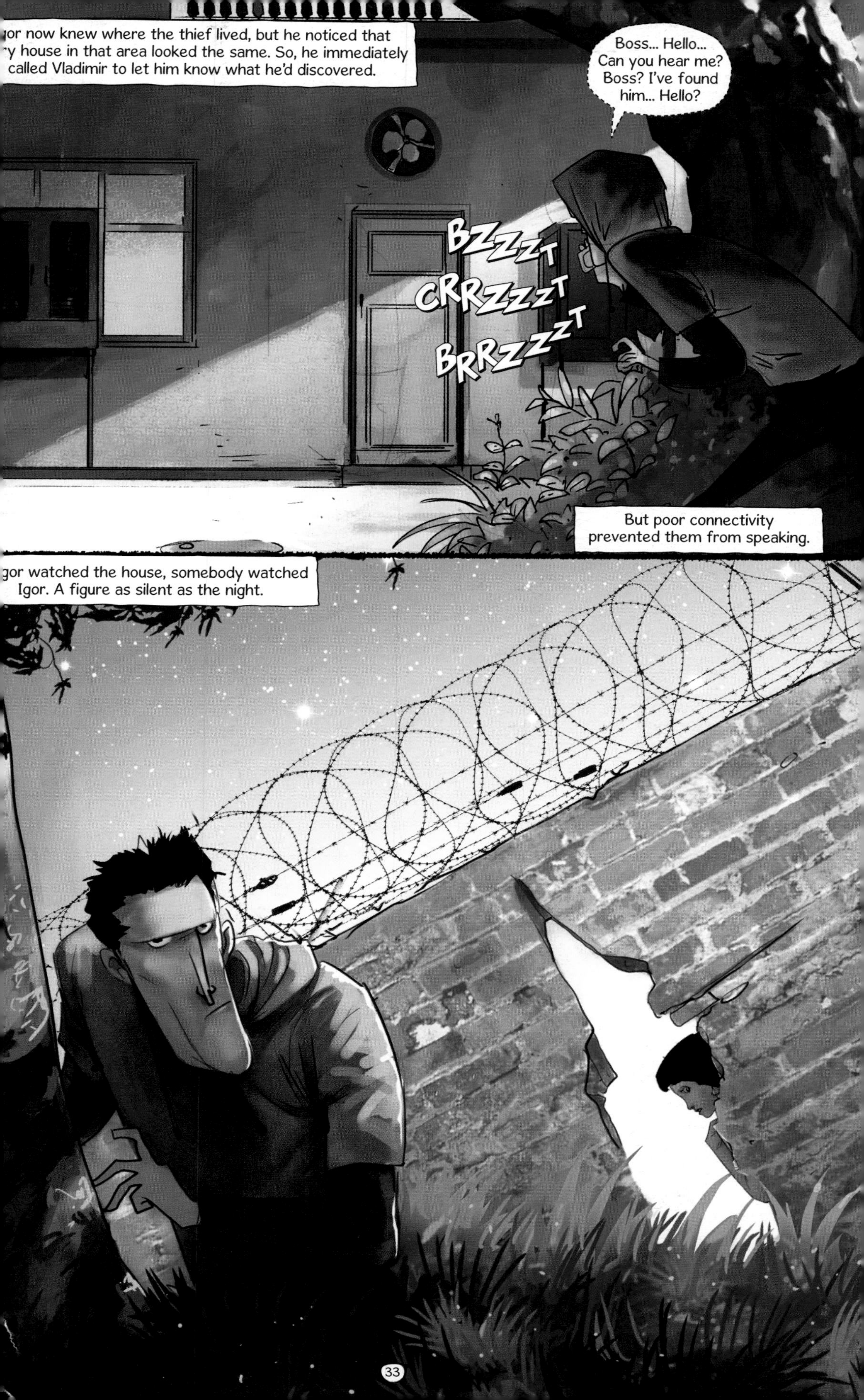
gor now knew where the thief lived, but he noticed that
ry house in that area looked the same. So, he immediately
called Vladimir to let him know what he'd discovered.
Boss... Hello... Can you hear me? Boss? I've found him... Hello?
BZZZZT
CRRZZZZT
BRRZZZZT
But poor connectivity prevented them from speaking.
gor watched the house, somebody watched Igor. A figure as silent as the night.

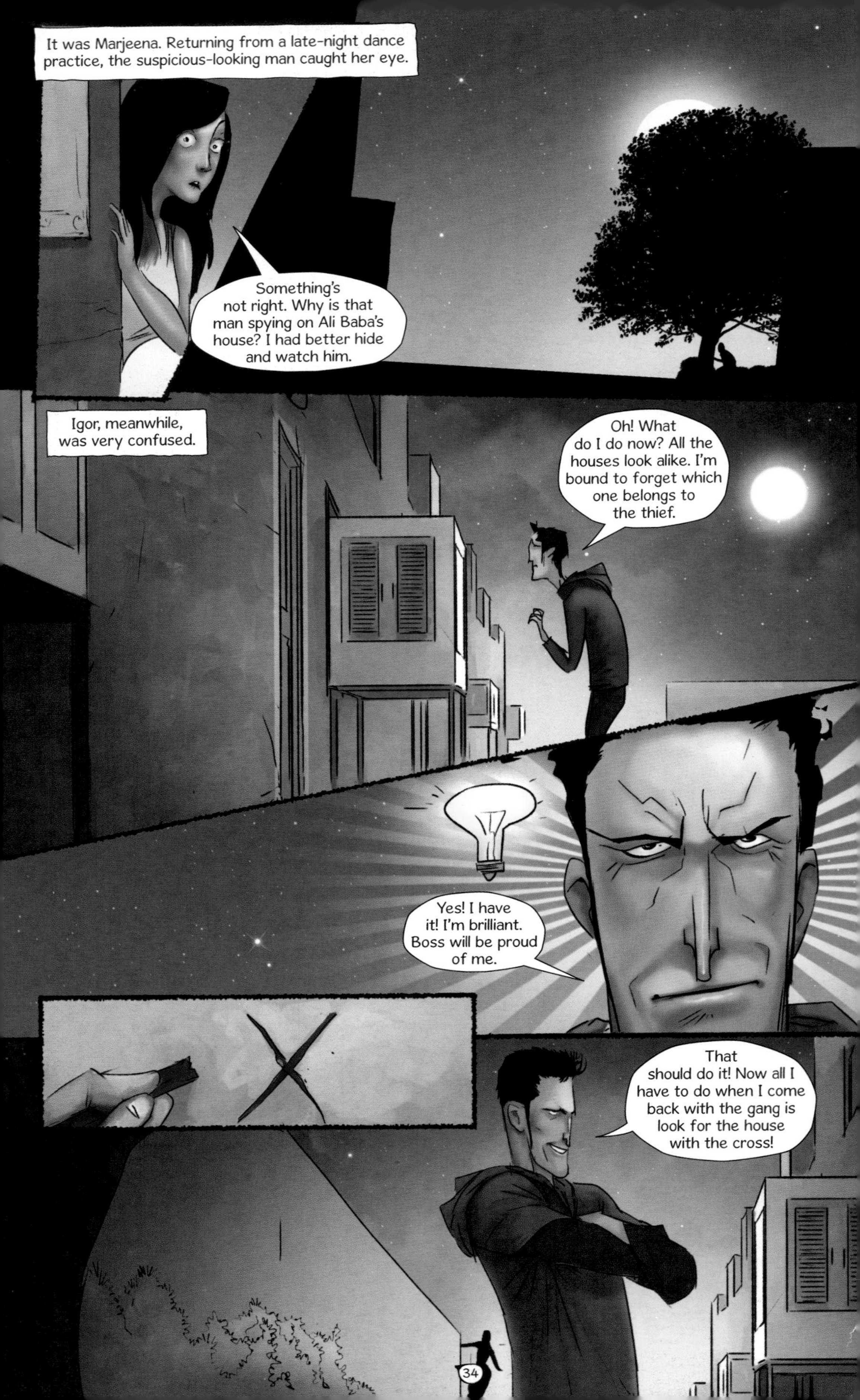
It was Marjeena. Returning from a late-night dance practice, the suspicious-looking man caught her eye.
Something's not right. Why is that man spying on Ali Baba's house? I had better hide and watch him.
Igor, meanwhile, was very confused.
Oh! What do I do now? All the houses look alike. I'm bound to forget which one belongs to the thief.
Yes! I have it! I'm brilliant. Boss will be proud of me.
That should do it! Now all I have to do when I come back with the gang is look for the house with the cross!

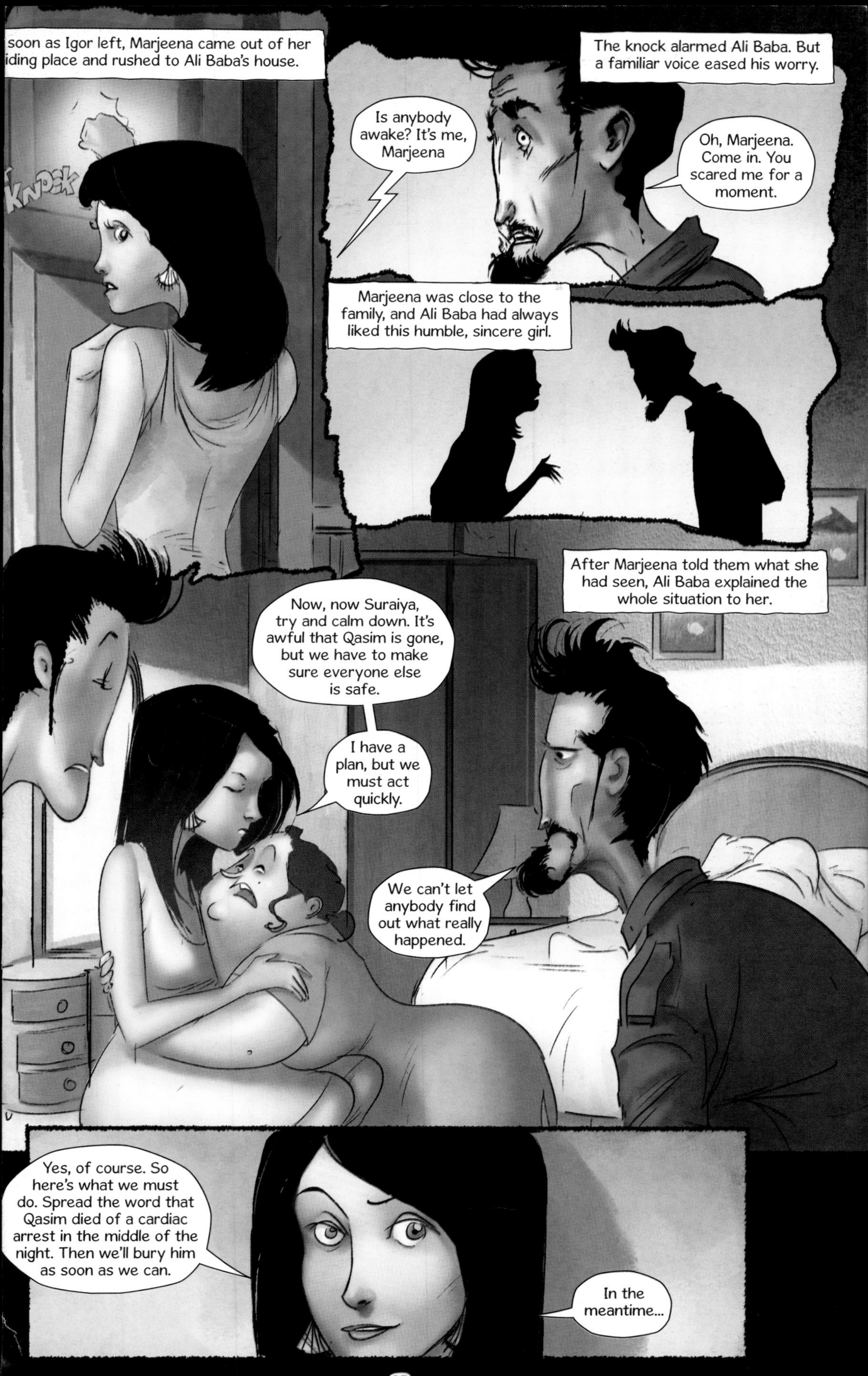
soon as Igor left, Marjeena came out of her iding place and rushed to Ali Baba's house.
KNOCK
The knock alarmed Ali Baba. But a familiar voice eased his worry.
Is anybody awake? It's me, Marjeena
Oh, Marjeena. Come in. You scared me for a moment.
Marjeena was close to the family, and Ali Baba had always liked this humble, sincere girl.
After Marjeena told them what she had seen, Ali Baba explained the whole situation to her.
Now, now Suraiya, try and calm down. It's awful that Qasim is gone, but we have to make sure everyone else is safe.
I have a plan, but we must act quickly.
We can't let anybody find out what really happened.
Yes, of course. So here's what we must do. Spread the word that Qasim died of a cardiac arrest in the middle of the night. Then we'll bury him as soon as we can.
In the meantime...

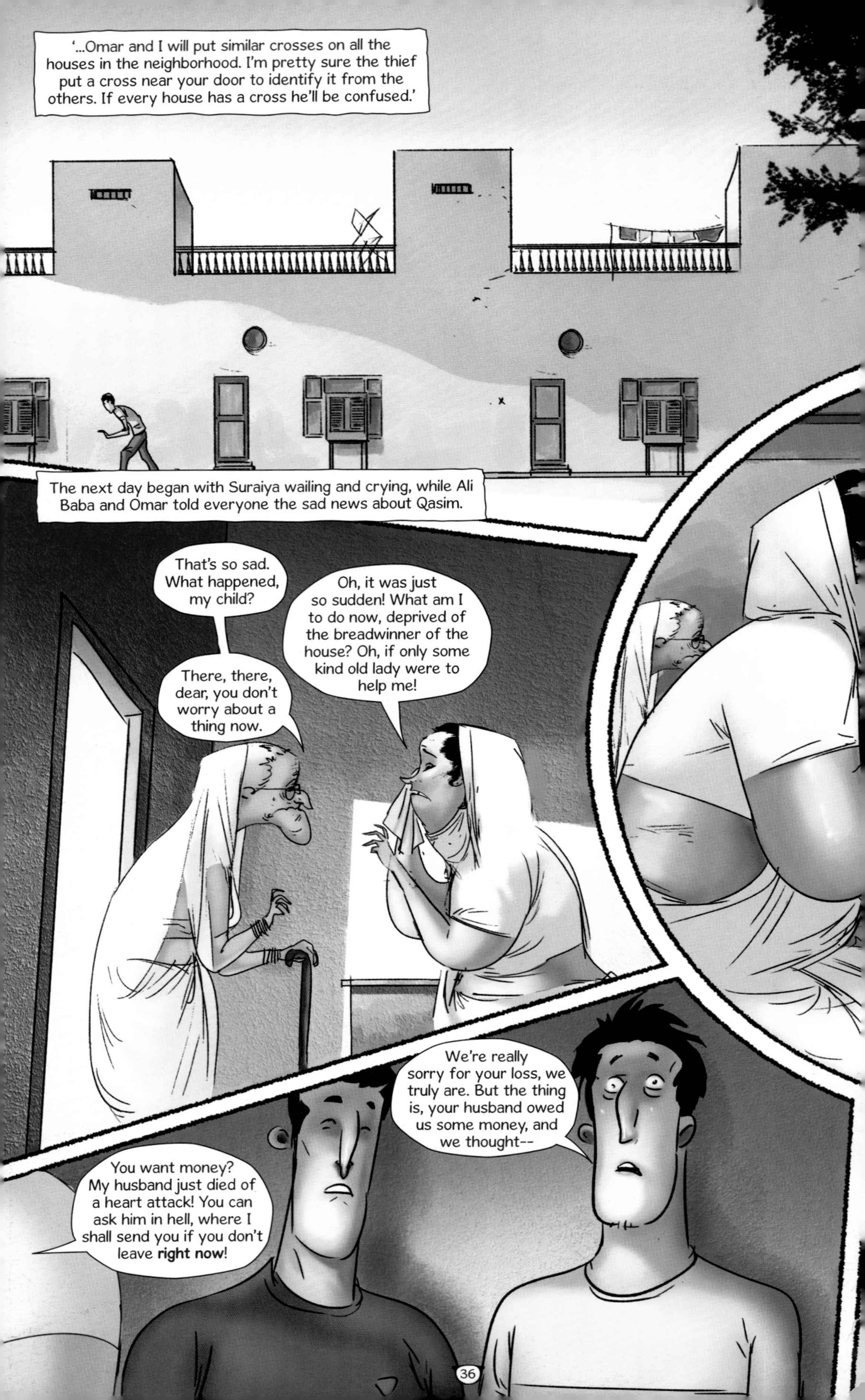
'...Omar and I will put similar crosses on all the houses in the neighborhood. I'm pretty sure the thief put a cross near your door to identify it from the others. If every house has a cross he'll be confused.'
The next day began with Suraiya wailing and crying, while Ali Baba and Omar told everyone the sad news about Qasim.
That's so sad. What happened, my child?
Oh, it was just so sudden! What am I to do now, deprived of the breadwinner of the house? Oh, if only some kind old lady were to help me!
There, there, dear, you don't worry about a thing now.
We're really sorry for your loss, we truly are. But the thing is, your husband owed us some money, and we thought--
You want money? My husband just died of a heart attack! You can ask him in hell, where I shall send you if you don't leave **right now**!

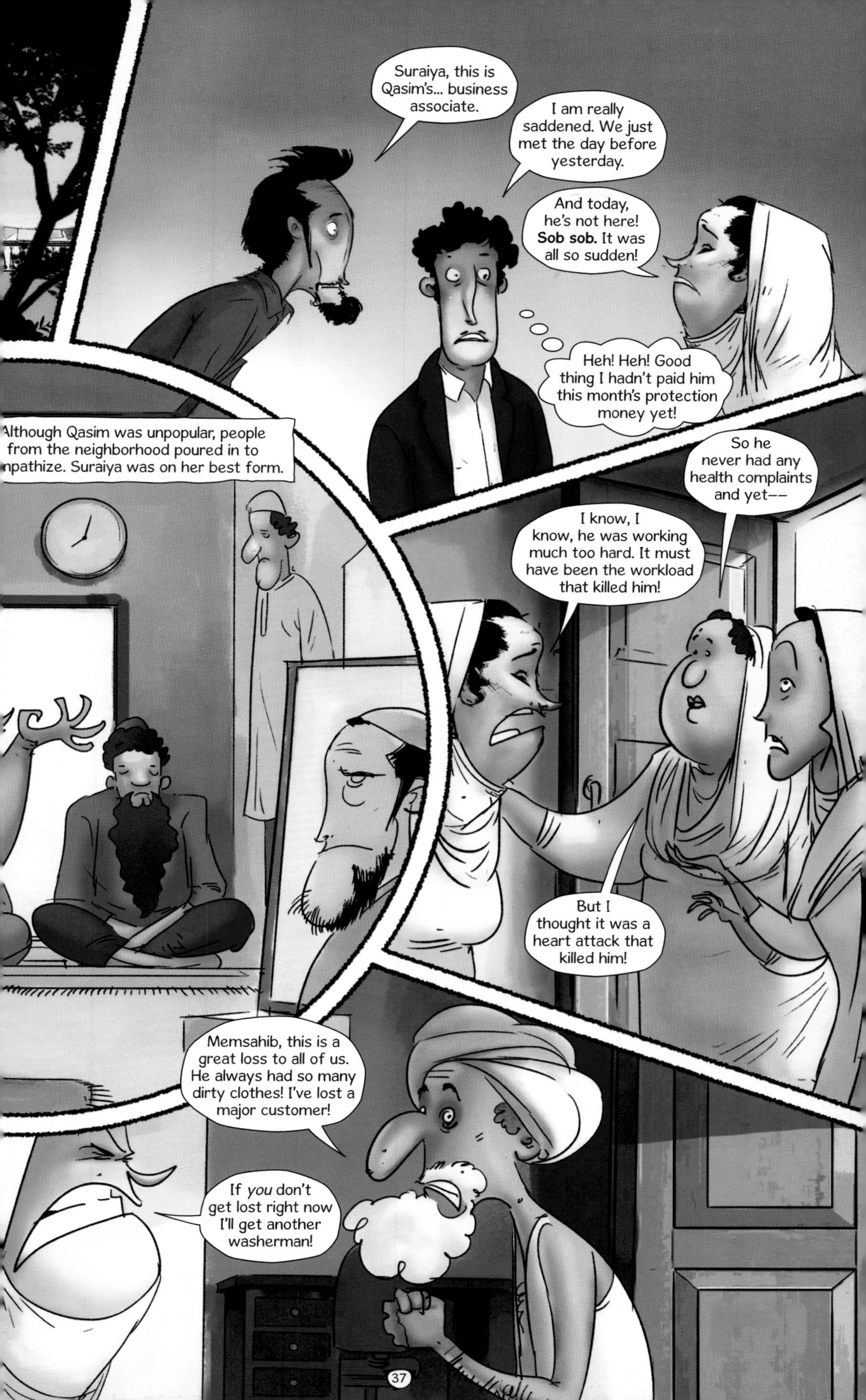
Suraiya, this is Qasim's... business associate.
I am really saddened. We just met the day before yesterday.
And today, he's not here! **Sob sob.** It was all so sudden!
Heh! Heh! Good thing I hadn't paid him this month's protection money yet!
Although Qasim was unpopular, people from the neighborhood poured in to
npathize. Suraiya was on her best form.
So he never had any health complaints and yet--
I know, I know, he was working much too hard. It must have been the workload that killed him!
But I thought it was a heart attack that killed him!
Memsahib, this is a great loss to all of us. He always had so many dirty clothes! I've lost a major customer!
If *you* don't get lost right now I'll get another washerman!

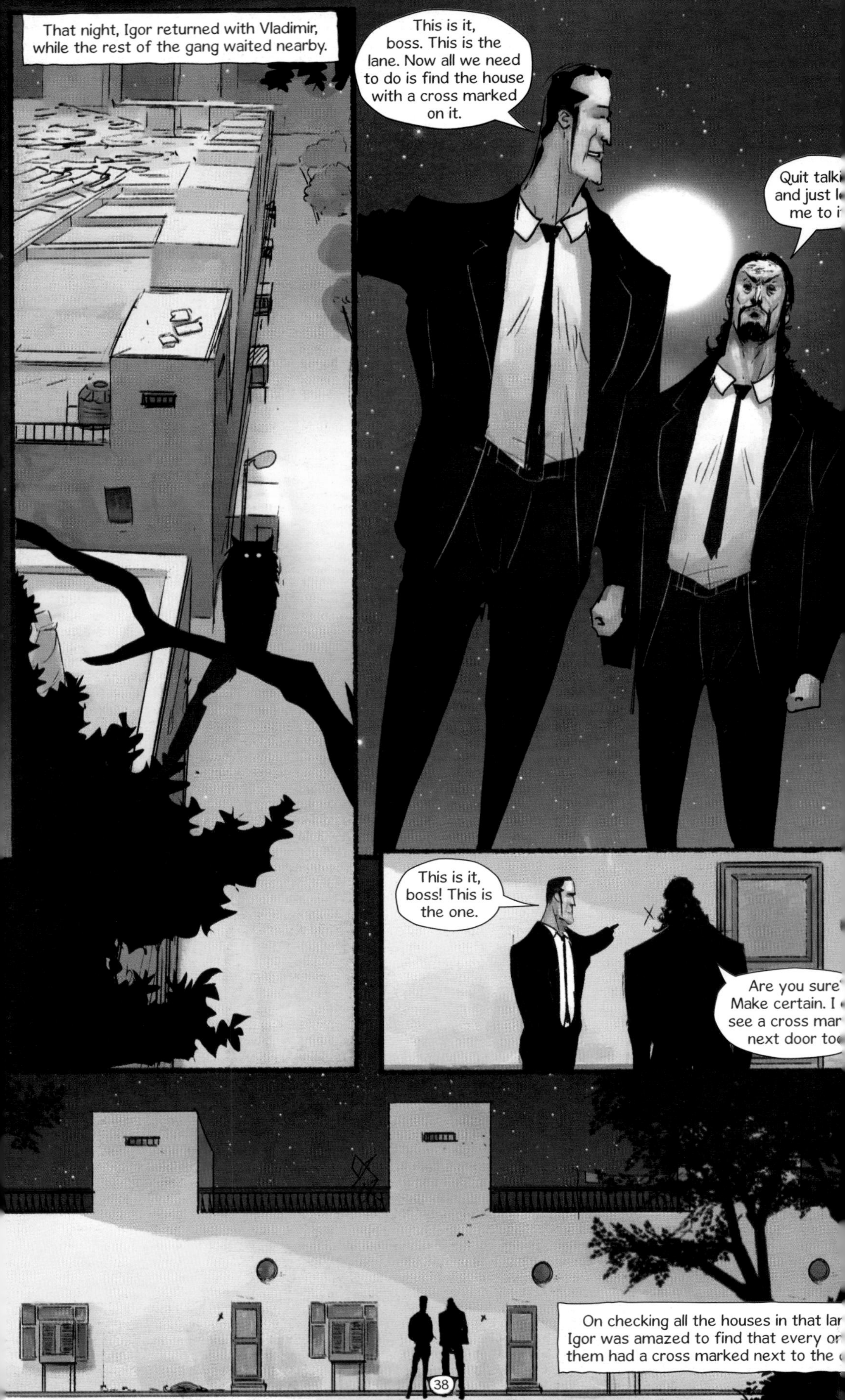
That night, Igor returned with Vladimir, while the rest of the gang waited nearby.
This is it, boss. This is the lane. Now all we need to do is find the house with a cross marked on it.
Quit talki and just l me to i
This is it, boss! This is the one.
Are you sure Make certain. I see a cross mar next door to
On checking all the houses in that lar Igor was amazed to find that every of them had a cross marked next to the

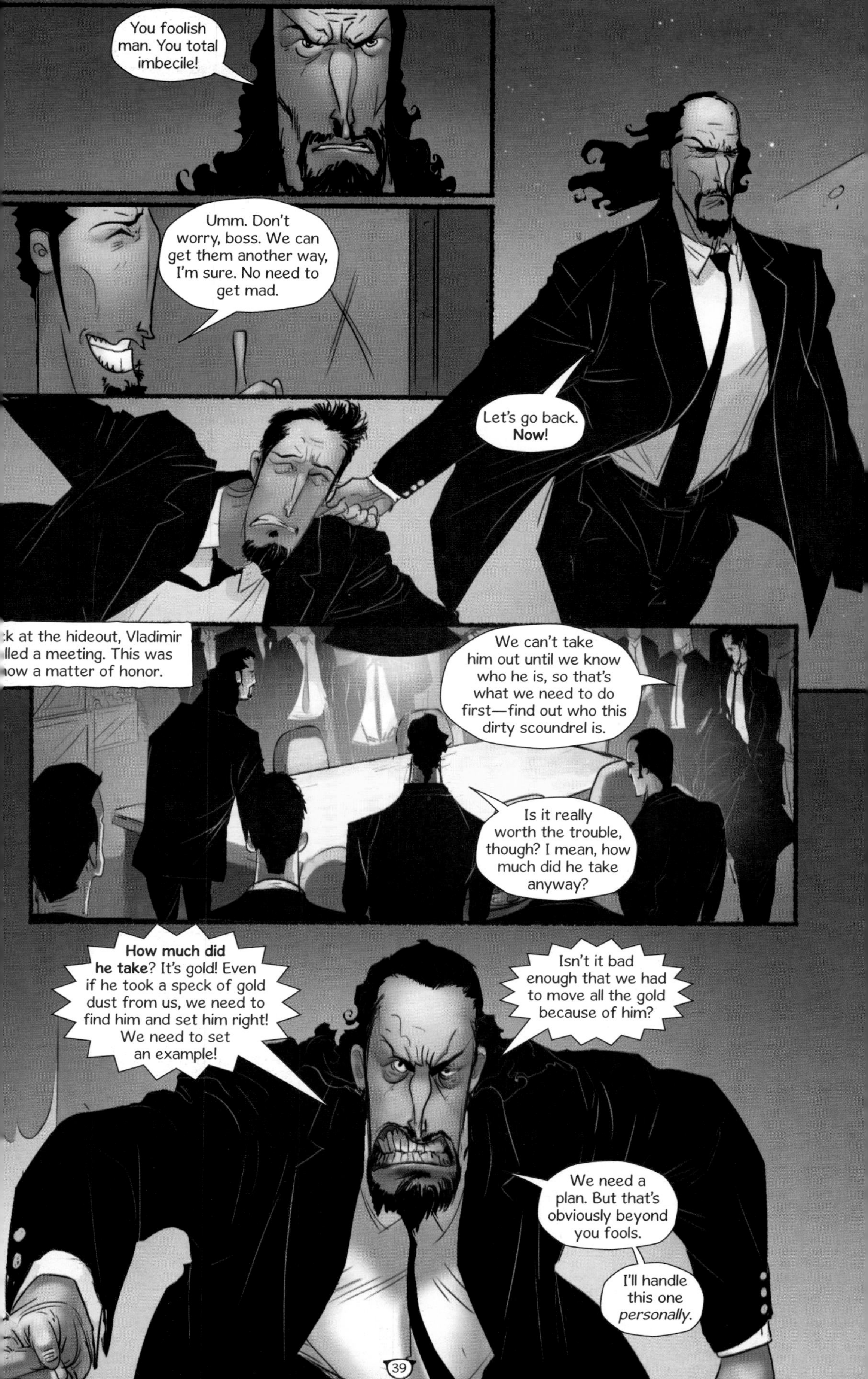
You foolish man. You total imbecile!
Umm. Don't worry, boss. We can get them another way, I'm sure. No need to get mad.
Let's go back. **Now!**
...k at the hideout, Vladimir ...lled a meeting. This was ...ow a matter of honor.
We can't take him out until we know who he is, so that's what we need to do first—find out who this dirty scoundrel is.
Is it really worth the trouble, though? I mean, how much did he take anyway?
How much did he take? It's gold! Even if he took a speck of gold dust from us, we need to find him and set him right! We need to set an example!
Isn't it bad enough that we had to move all the gold because of him?
We need a plan. But that's obviously beyond you fools.
I'll handle this one *personally*.

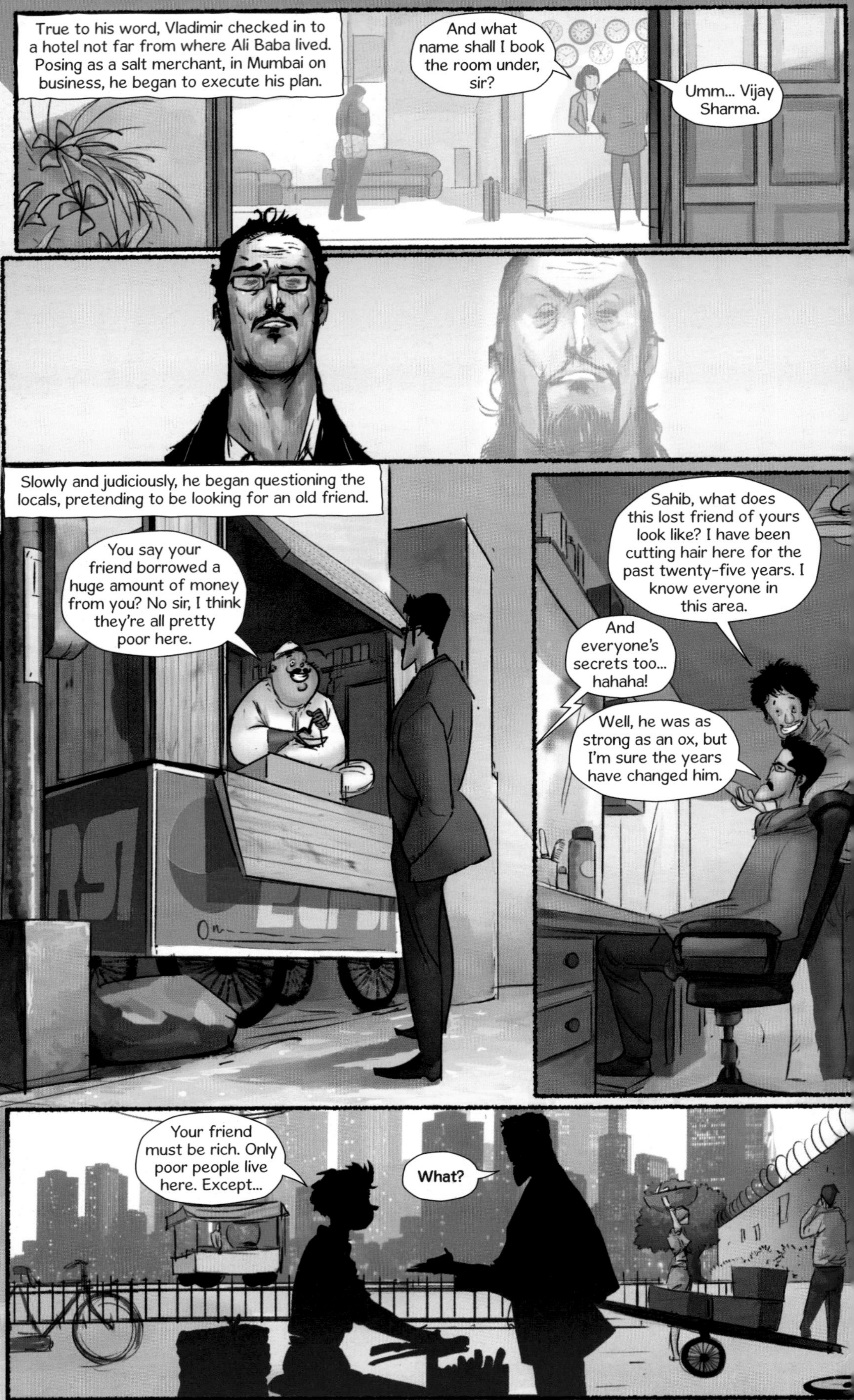
True to his word, Vladimir checked in to a hotel not far from where Ali Baba lived. Posing as a salt merchant, in Mumbai on business, he began to execute his plan.
And what name shall I book the room under, sir?
Umm... Vijay Sharma.
Slowly and judiciously, he began questioning the locals, pretending to be looking for an old friend.
You say your friend borrowed a huge amount of money from you? No sir, I think they're all pretty poor here.
Sahib, what does this lost friend of yours look like? I have been cutting hair here for the past twenty-five years. I know everyone in this area.
And everyone's secrets too... hahaha!
Well, he was as strong as an ox, but I'm sure the years have changed him.
Your friend must be rich. Only poor people live here. Except...
What?

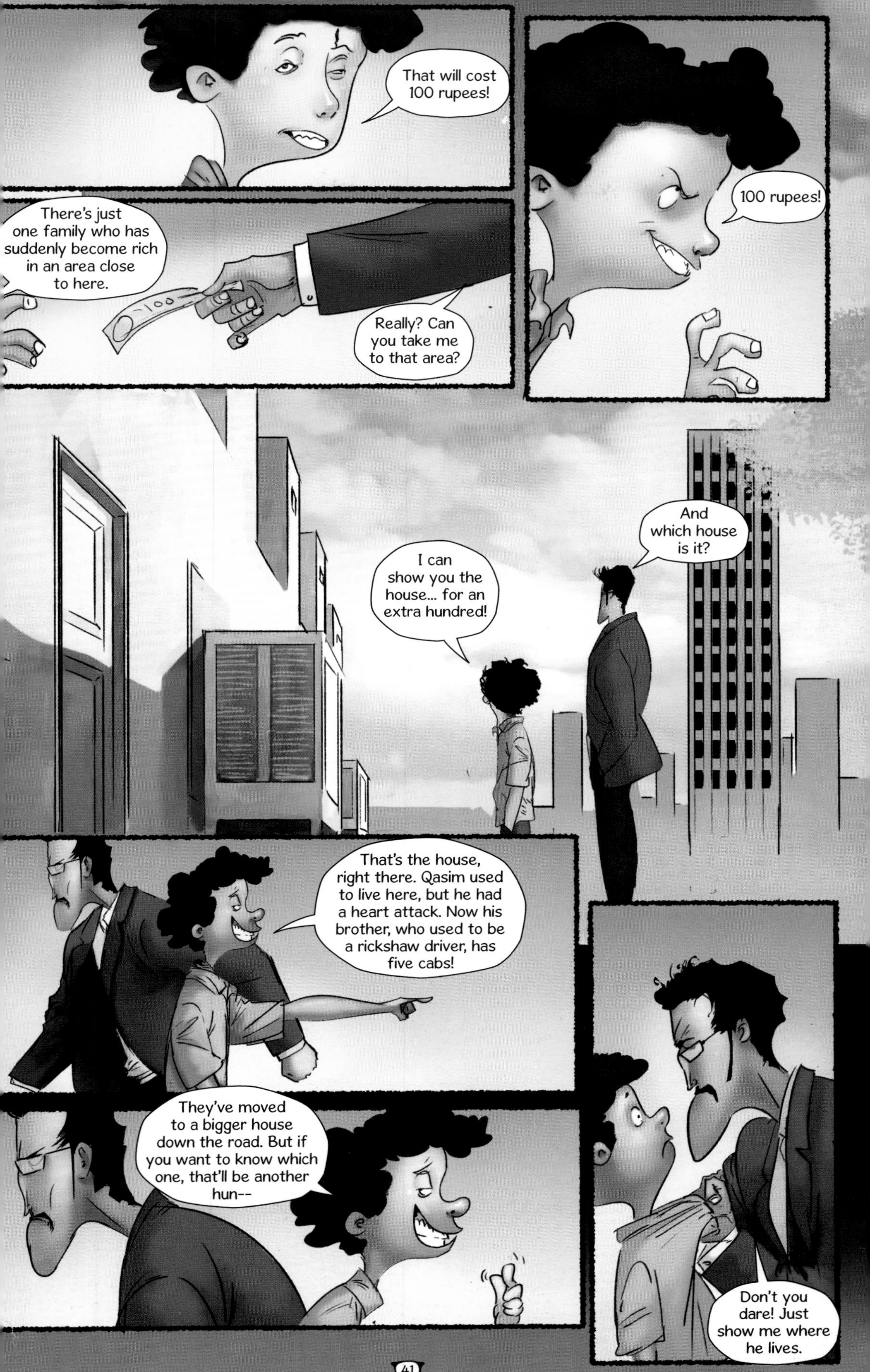

That will cost 100 rupees!
There's just one family who has suddenly become rich in an area close to here.
Really? Can you take me to that area?
100 rupees!
I can show you the house... for an extra hundred!
And which house is it?
That's the house, right there. Qasim used to live here, but he had a heart attack. Now his brother, who used to be a rickshaw driver, has five cabs!
They've moved to a bigger house down the road. But if you want to know which one, that'll be another hun--
Don't you dare! Just show me where he lives.

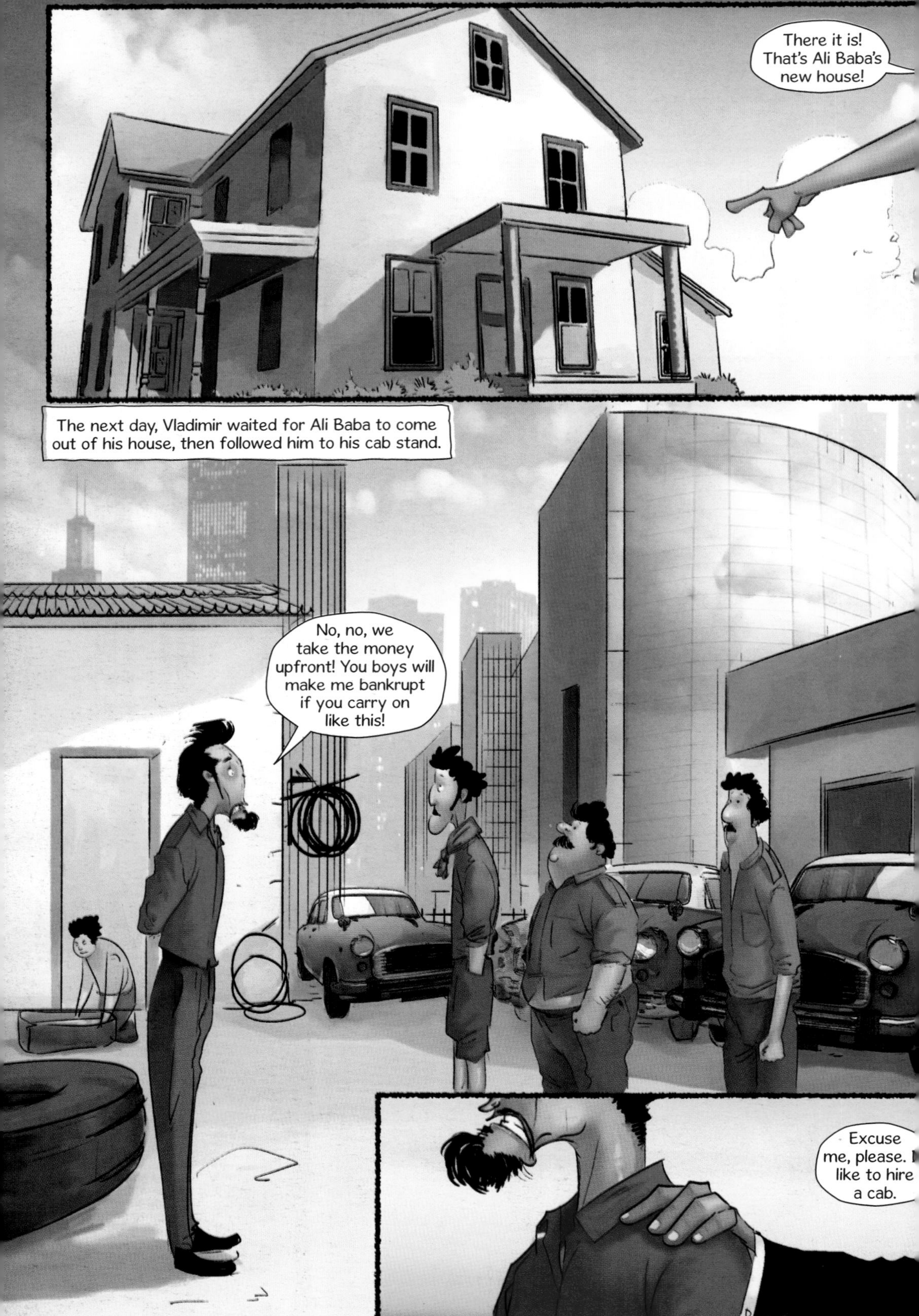
There it is! That's Ali Baba's new house!
The next day, Vladimir waited for Ali Baba to come out of his house, then followed him to his cab stand.
No, no, we take the money upfront! You boys will make me bankrupt if you carry on like this!
Excuse me, please. I like to hire a cab.

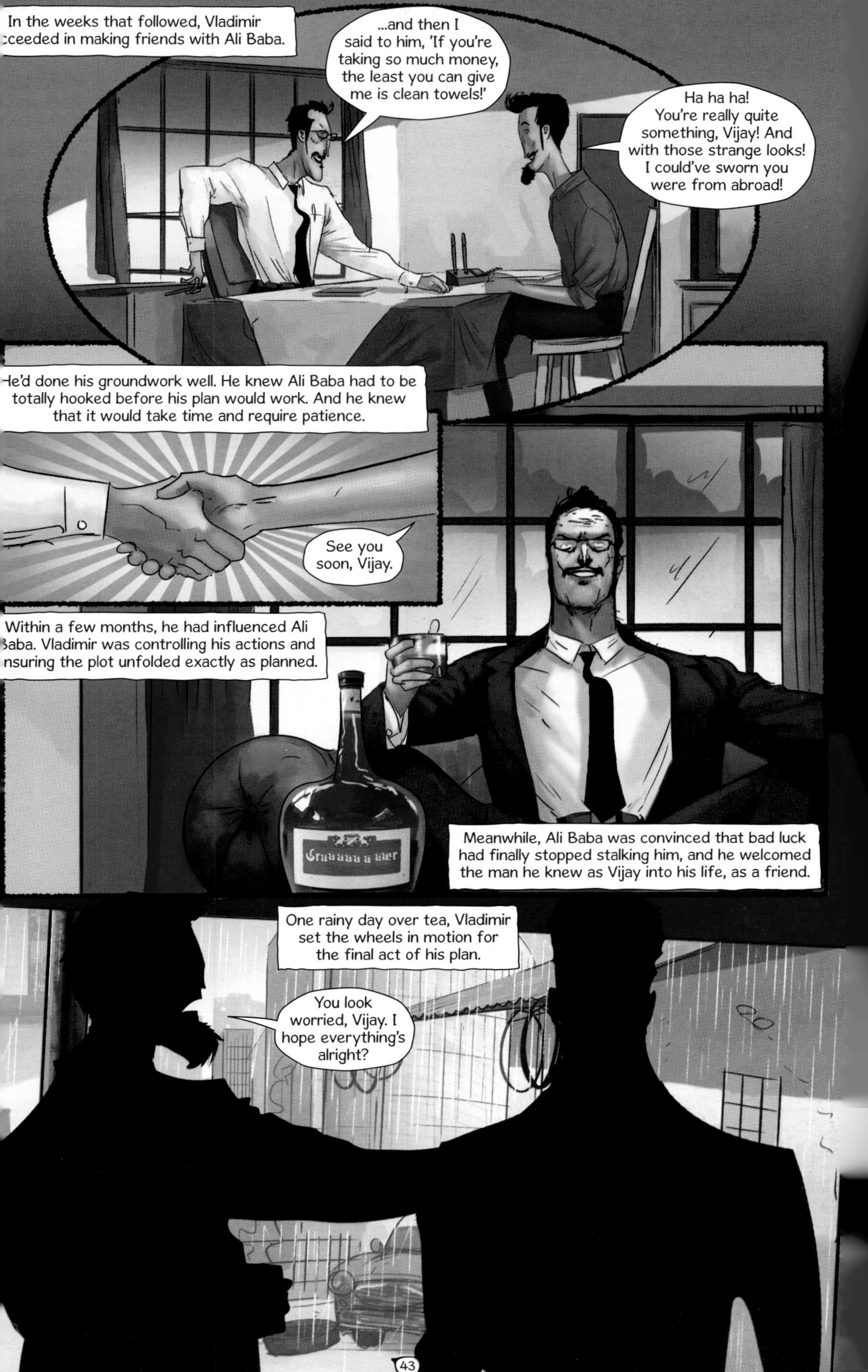
In the weeks that followed, Vladimir ceeded in making friends with Ali Baba.
...and then I said to him, 'If you're taking so much money, the least you can give me is clean towels!'
Ha ha ha! You're really quite something, Vijay! And with those strange looks! I could've sworn you were from abroad!
e'd done his groundwork well. He knew Ali Baba had to be totally hooked before his plan would work. And he knew that it would take time and require patience.
See you soon, Vijay.
Within a few months, he had influenced Ali aba. Vladimir was controlling his actions and nsuring the plot unfolded exactly as planned.
Meanwhile, Ali Baba was convinced that bad luck had finally stopped stalking him, and he welcomed the man he knew as Vijay into his life, as a friend.
One rainy day over tea, Vladimir set the wheels in motion for the final act of his plan.
You look worried, Vijay. I hope everything's alright?

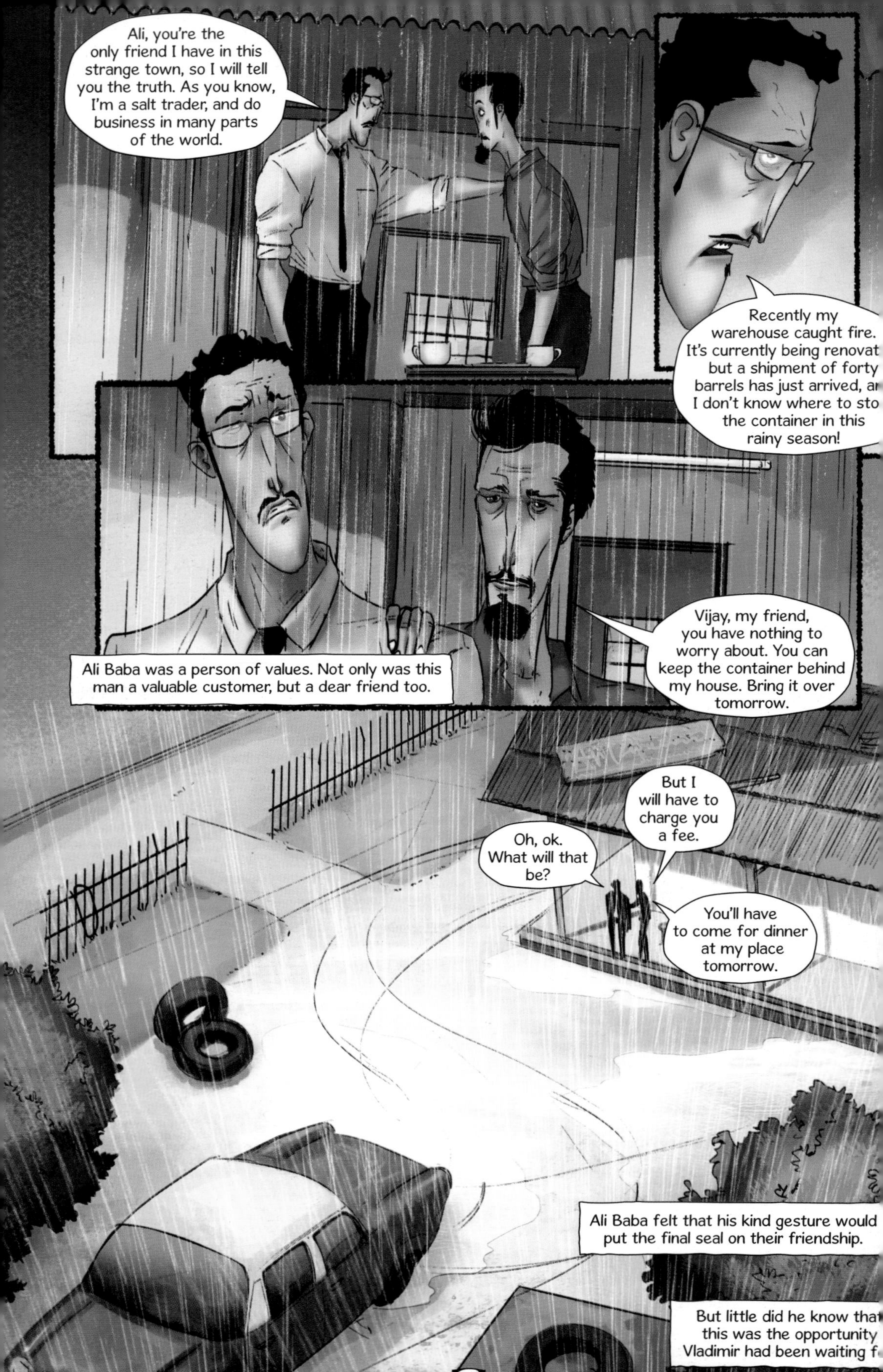
Ali, you're the only friend I have in this strange town, so I will tell you the truth. As you know, I'm a salt trader, and do business in many parts of the world.
Recently my warehouse caught fire. It's currently being renovat
but a shipment of forty barrels has just arrived, a
I don't know where to sto
the container in this rainy season!
Ali Baba was a person of values. Not only was this man a valuable customer, but a dear friend too.
Vijay, my friend, you have nothing to worry about. You can keep the container behind my house. Bring it over tomorrow.
But I will have to charge you a fee.
Oh, ok. What will that be?
You'll have to come for dinner at my place tomorrow.
Ali Baba felt that his kind gesture would put the final seal on their friendship.
But little did he know tha
this was the opportunity
Vladimir had been waiting f

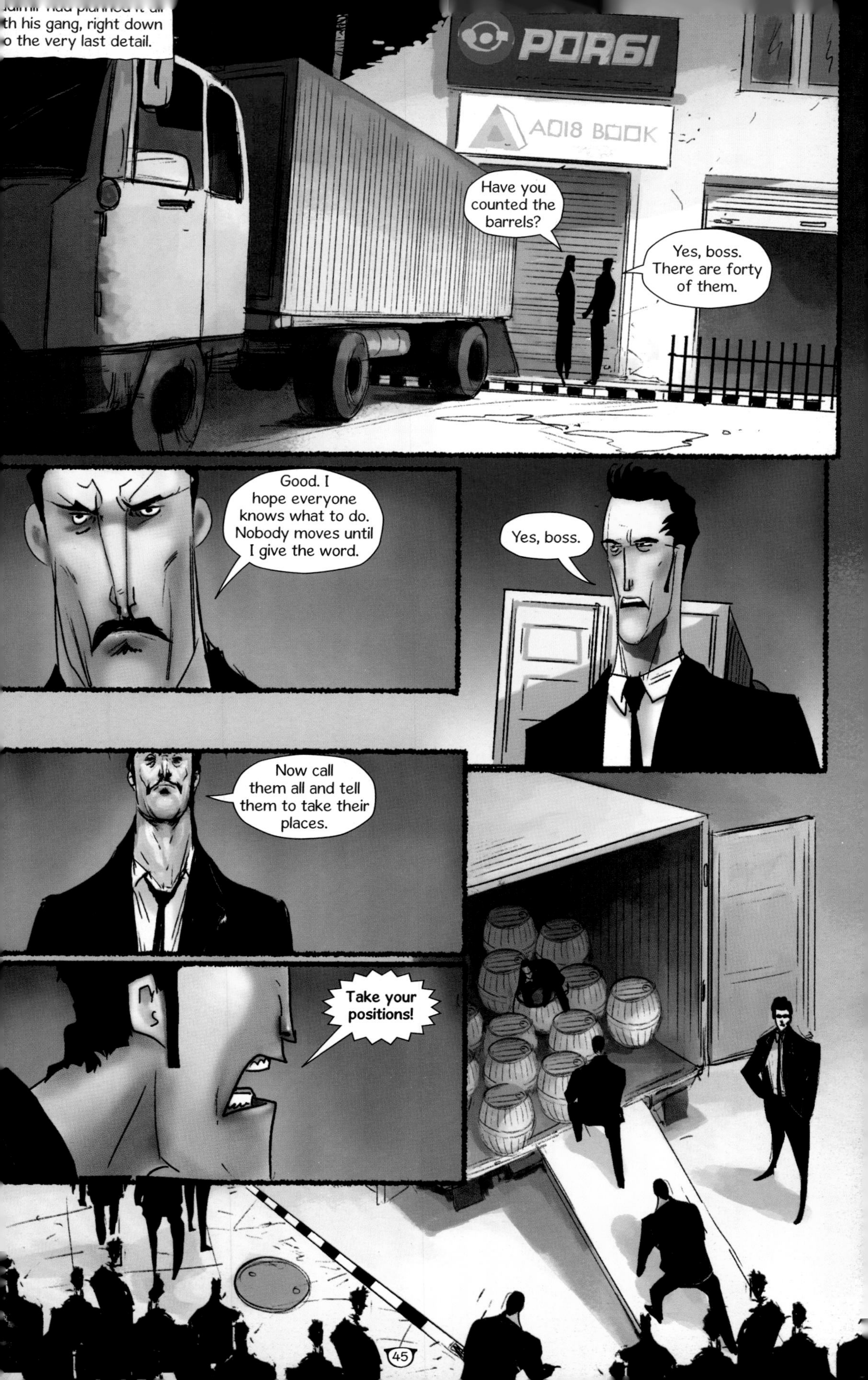

...dimir had planned it all ...th his gang, right down ...o the very last detail.
PORGI
ADI8 BOOK
Have you counted the barrels?
Yes, boss. There are forty of them.
Good. I hope everyone knows what to do. Nobody moves until I give the word.
Yes, boss.
Now call them all and tell them to take their places.
Take your positions!

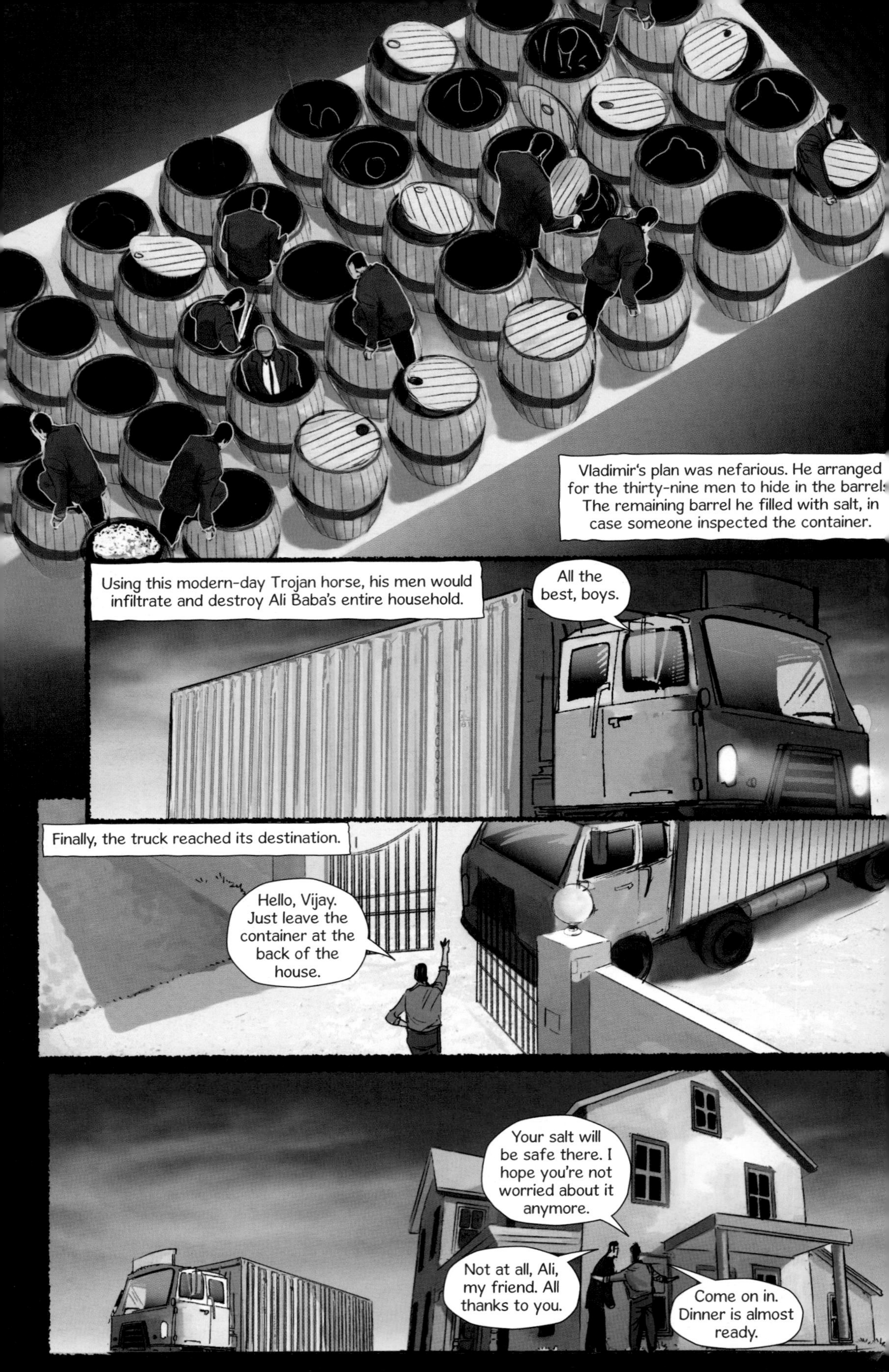
Vladimir's plan was nefarious. He arranged for the thirty-nine men to hide in the barrel
The remaining barrel he filled with salt, in case someone inspected the container.
Using this modern-day Trojan horse, his men would infiltrate and destroy Ali Baba's entire household.
All the best, boys.
Finally, the truck reached its destination.
Hello, Vijay. Just leave the container at the back of the house.
Your salt will be safe there. I hope you're not worried about it anymore.
Not at all, Ali, my friend. All thanks to you.
Come on in. Dinner is almost ready.

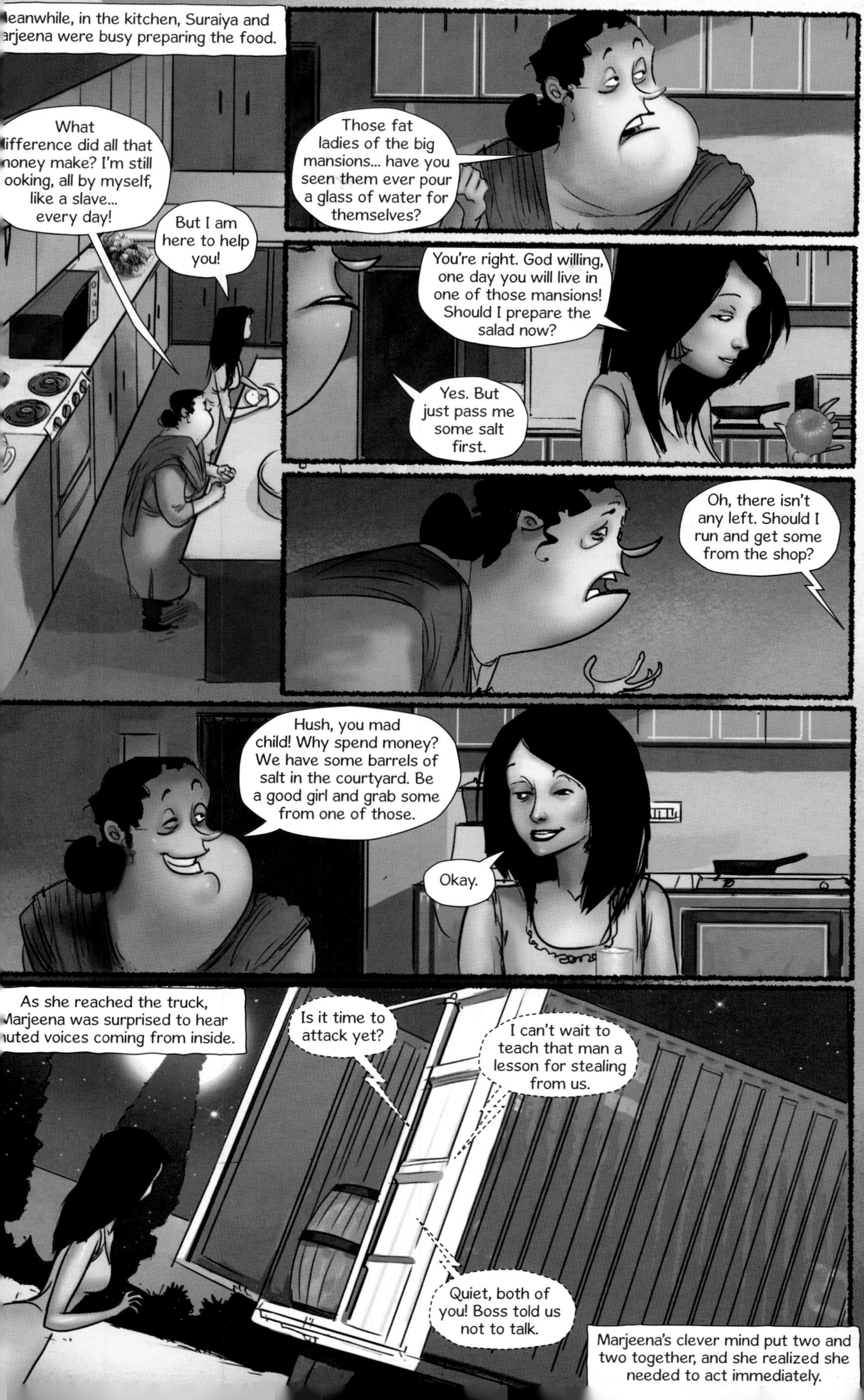
eanwhile, in the kitchen, Suraiya and
arjeena were busy preparing the food.
What ifference did all that noney make? I'm still ooking, all by myself, like a slave... every day!
But I am here to help you!
Those fat ladies of the big mansions... have you seen them ever pour a glass of water for themselves?
You're right. God willing, one day you will live in one of those mansions! Should I prepare the salad now?
Yes. But just pass me some salt first.
Oh, there isn't any left. Should I run and get some from the shop?
Hush, you mad child! Why spend money? We have some barrels of salt in the courtyard. Be a good girl and grab some from one of those.
Okay.
As she reached the truck, Marjeena was surprised to hear uted voices coming from inside.
Is it time to attack yet?
I can't wait to teach that man a lesson for stealing from us.
Quiet, both of you! Boss told us not to talk.
Marjeena's clever mind put two and two together, and she realized she needed to act immediately.

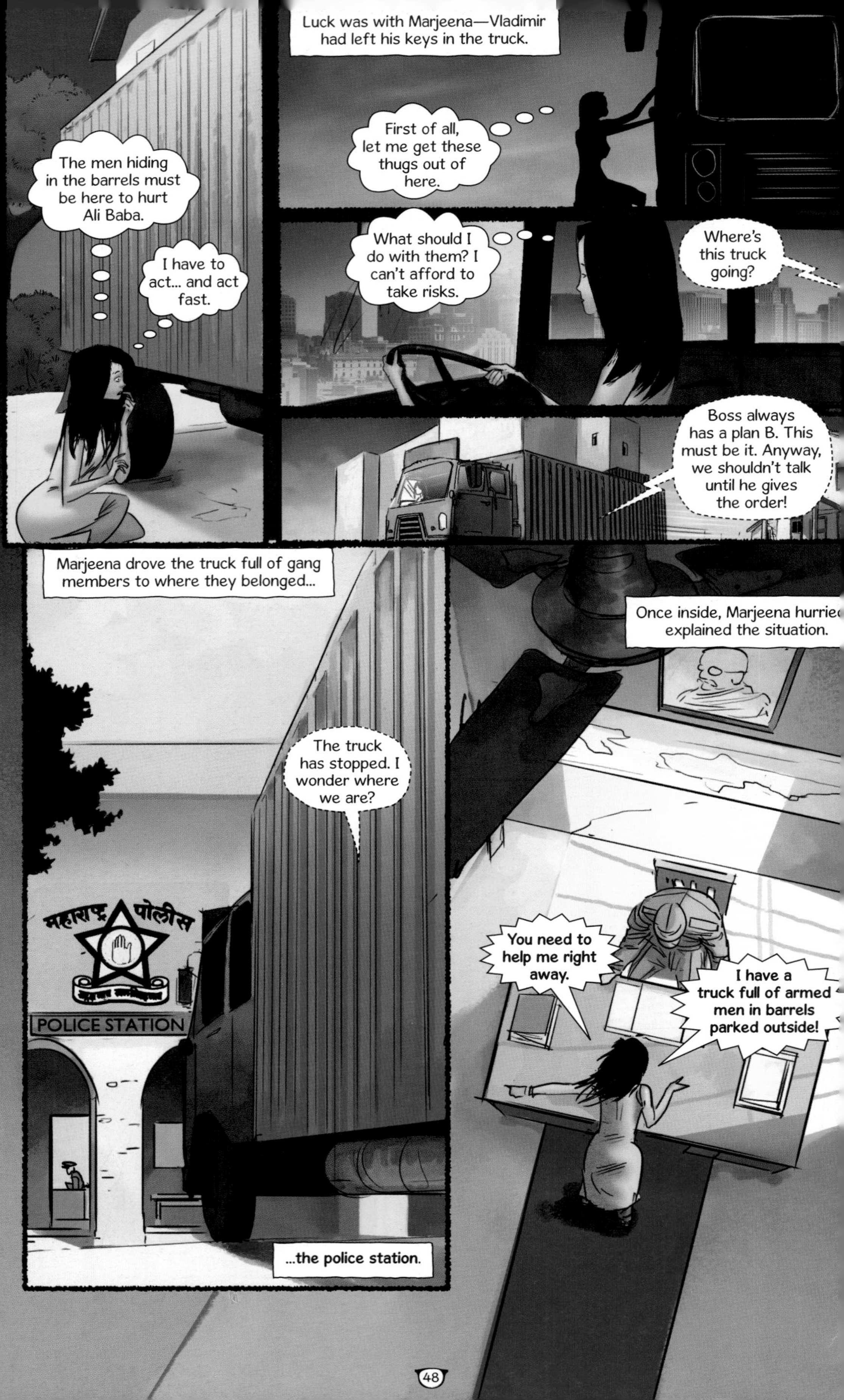

Luck was with Marjeena—Vladimir had left his keys in the truck.
The men hiding in the barrels must be here to hurt Ali Baba.
I have to act... and act fast.
First of all, let me get these thugs out of here.
What should I do with them? I can't afford to take risks.
Where's this truck going?
Boss always has a plan B. This must be it. Anyway, we shouldn't talk until he gives the order!
Marjeena drove the truck full of gang members to where they belonged...
The truck has stopped. I wonder where we are?
POLICE STATION
...the police station.
Once inside, Marjeena hurrie explained the situation.
You need to help me right away.
I have a truck full of armed men in barrels parked outside!

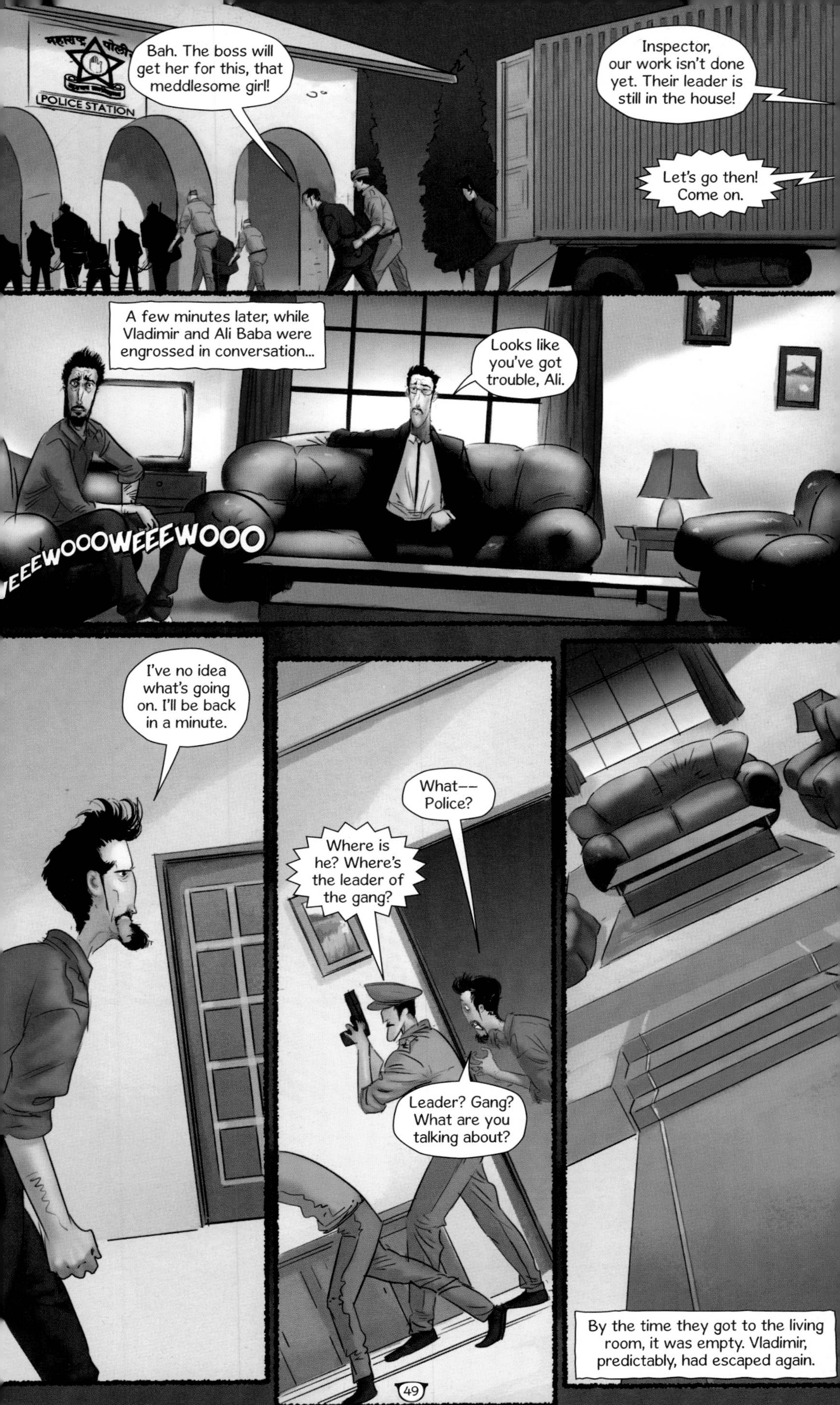
POLICE STATION
Bah. The boss will get her for this, that meddlesome girl!
Inspector, our work isn't done yet. Their leader is still in the house!
Let's go then! Come on.
A few minutes later, while Vladimir and Ali Baba were engrossed in conversation...
Looks like you've got trouble, Ali.
WEEEWOOOWEEEWOOO
I've no idea what's going on. I'll be back in a minute.
What-- Police?
Where is he? Where's the leader of the gang?
Leader? Gang? What are you talking about?
By the time they got to the living room, it was empty. Vladimir, predictably, had escaped again.

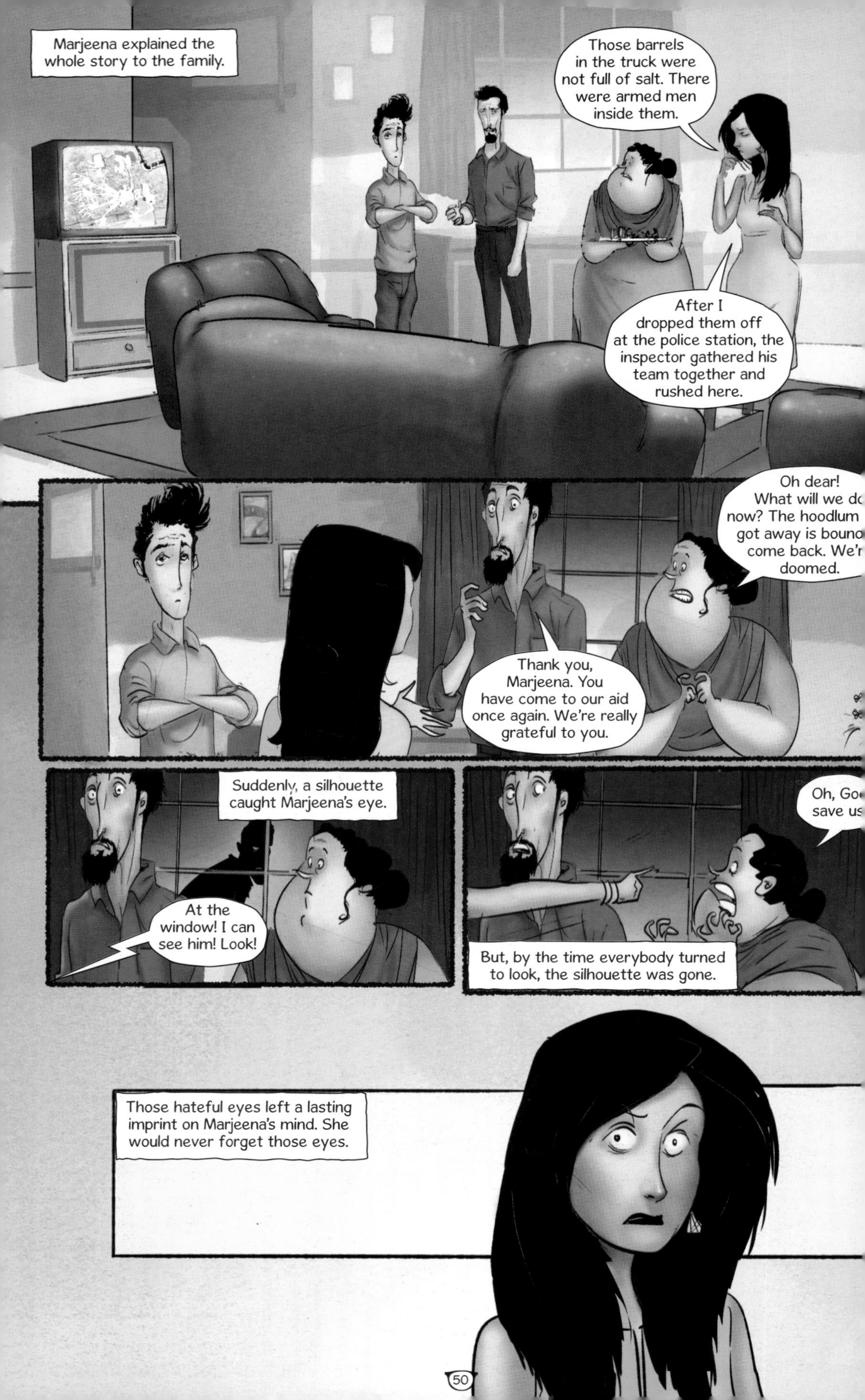
Marjeena explained the whole story to the family.
Those barrels in the truck were not full of salt. There were armed men inside them.
After I dropped them off at the police station, the inspector gathered his team together and rushed here.
Oh dear! What will we d now? The hoodlum got away is boun come back. We'r doomed.
Thank you, Marjeena. You have come to our aid once again. We're really grateful to you.
Suddenly, a silhouette caught Marjeena's eye.
At the window! I can see him! Look!
Oh, Go save us
But, by the time everybody turned to look, the silhouette was gone.
Those hateful eyes left a lasting imprint on Marjeena's mind. She would never forget those eyes.

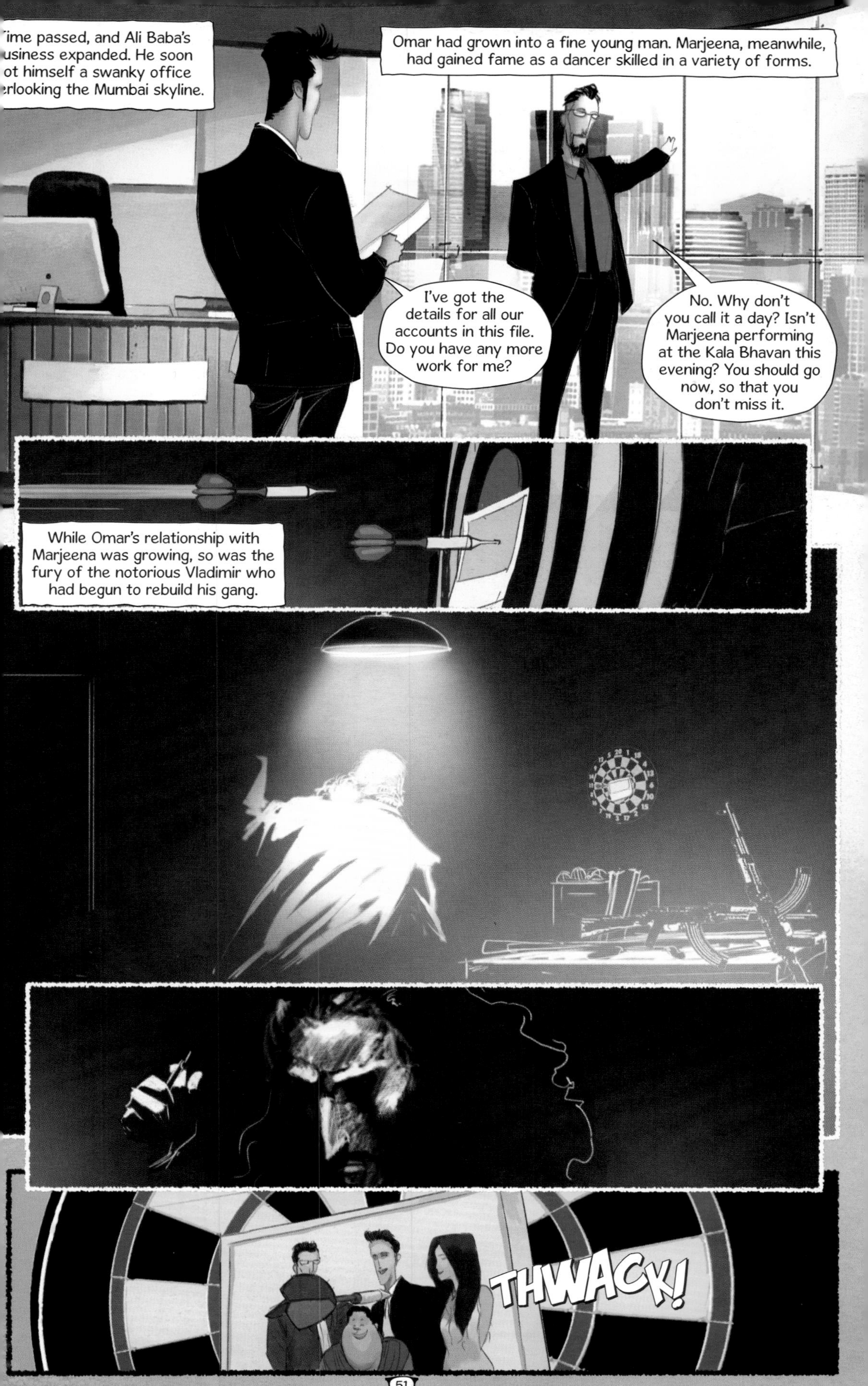

ime passed, and Ali Baba's usiness expanded. He soon ot himself a swanky office rlooking the Mumbai skyline.
Omar had grown into a fine young man. Marjeena, meanwhile, had gained fame as a dancer skilled in a variety of forms.
I've got the details for all our accounts in this file. Do you have any more work for me?
No. Why don't you call it a day? Isn't Marjeena performing at the Kala Bhavan this evening? You should go now, so that you don't miss it.
While Omar's relationship with Marjeena was growing, so was the fury of the notorious Vladimir who had begun to rebuild his gang.
THWACK!

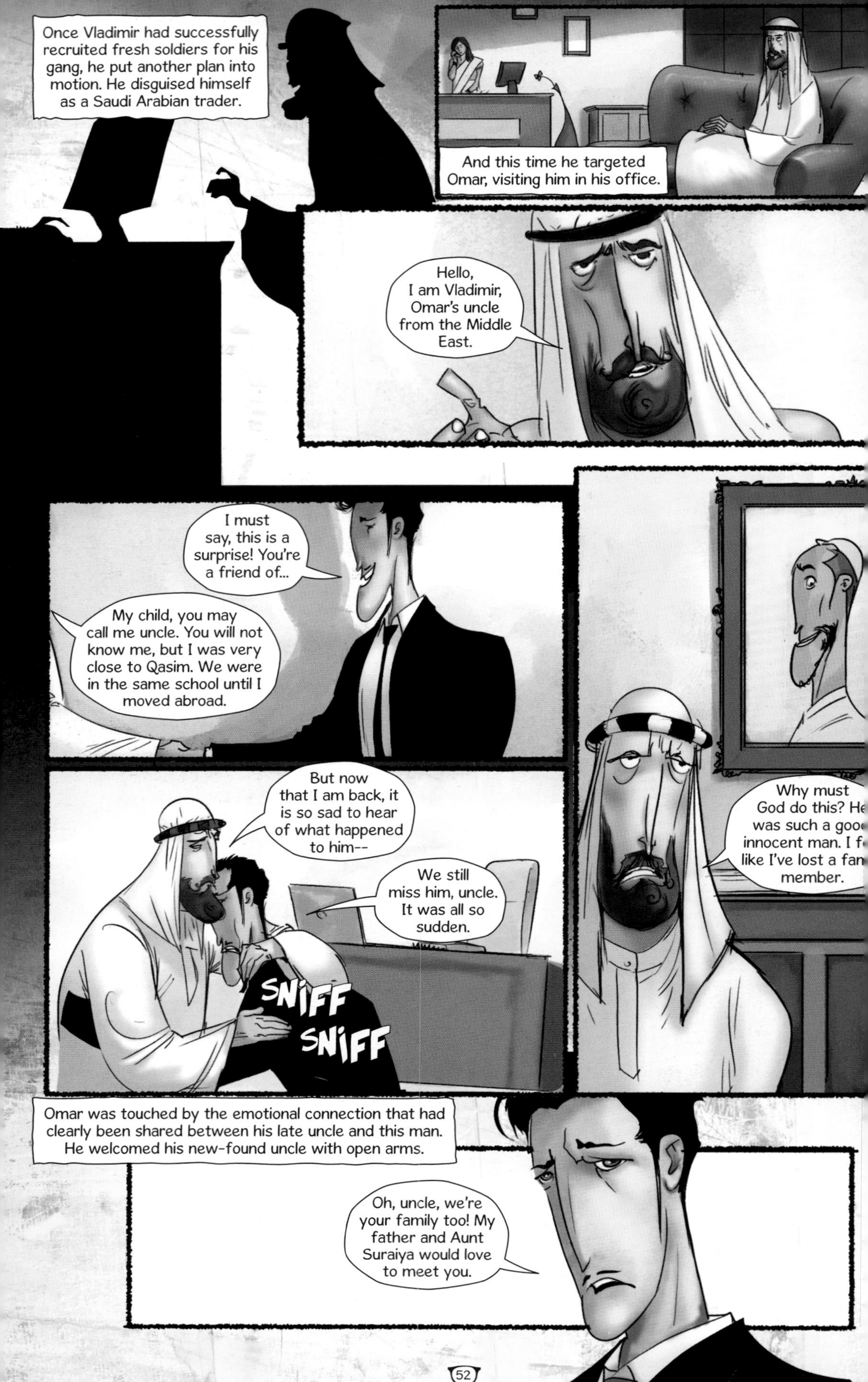

Once Vladimir had successfully recruited fresh soldiers for his gang, he put another plan into motion. He disguised himself as a Saudi Arabian trader.
And this time he targeted Omar, visiting him in his office.
Hello, I am Vladimir, Omar's uncle from the Middle East.
I must say, this is a surprise! You're a friend of...
My child, you may call me uncle. You will not know me, but I was very close to Qasim. We were in the same school until I moved abroad.
But now that I am back, it is so sad to hear of what happened to him--
We still miss him, uncle. It was all so sudden.
SNIFF SNIFF
Why must God do this? H was such a goo innocent man. I f like I've lost a fan member.
Omar was touched by the emotional connection that had clearly been shared between his late uncle and this man. He welcomed his new-found uncle with open arms.
Oh, uncle, we're your family too! My father and Aunt Suraiya would love to meet you.

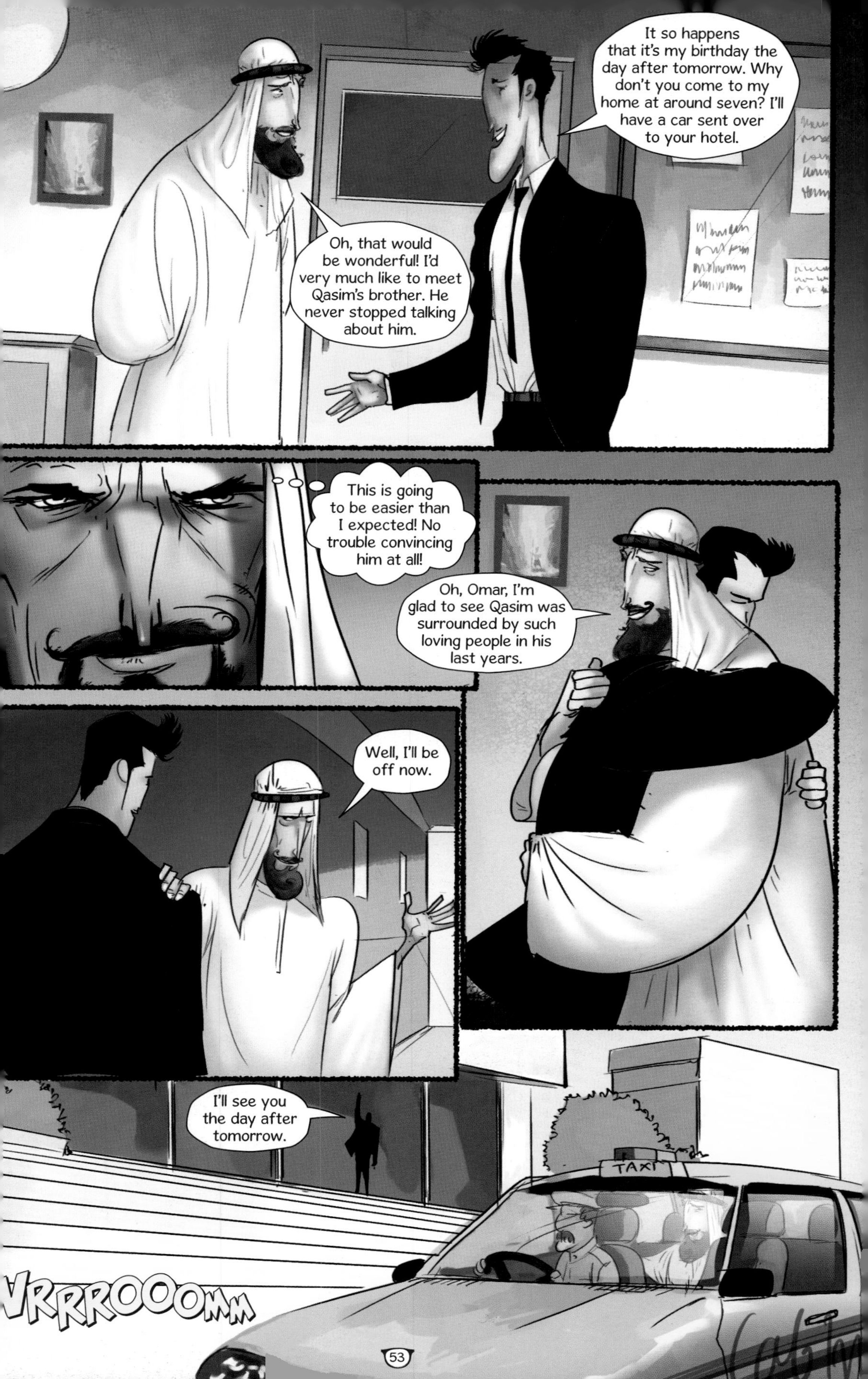

It so happens that it's my birthday the day after tomorrow. Why don't you come to my home at around seven? I'll have a car sent over to your hotel.
Oh, that would be wonderful! I'd very much like to meet Qasim's brother. He never stopped talking about him.
This is going to be easier than I expected! No trouble convincing him at all!
Oh, Omar, I'm glad to see Qasim was surrounded by such loving people in his last years.
Well, I'll be off now.
I'll see you the day after tomorrow.
TAXI
VRRROOOOMM

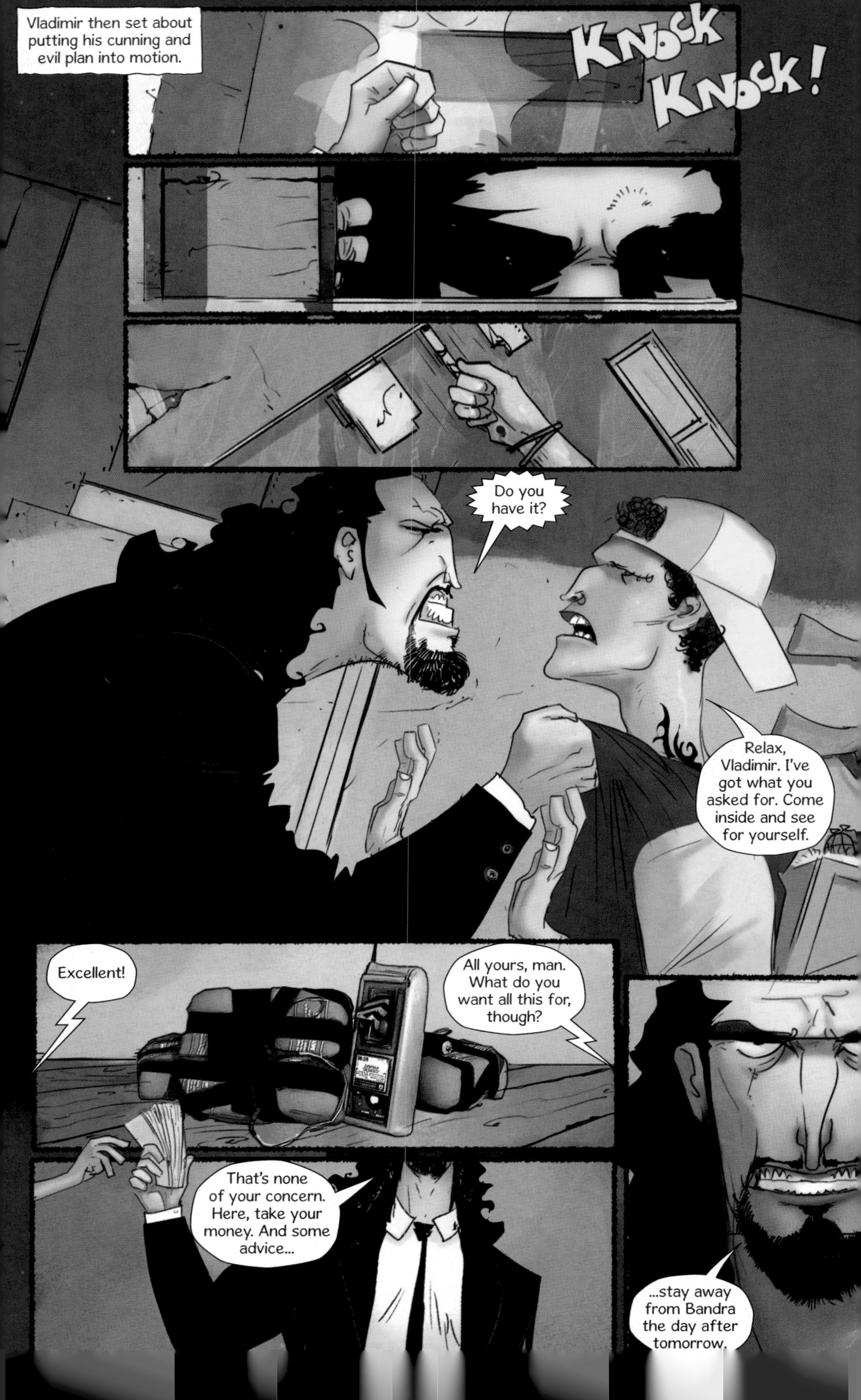
Vladimir then set about putting his cunning and evil plan into motion.
KNOCK KNOCK!
Do you have it?
Relax, Vladimir. I've got what you asked for. Come inside and see for yourself.
Excellent!
All yours, man. What do you want all this for, though?
That's none of your concern. Here, take your money. And some advice...
...stay away from Bandra the day after tomorrow.

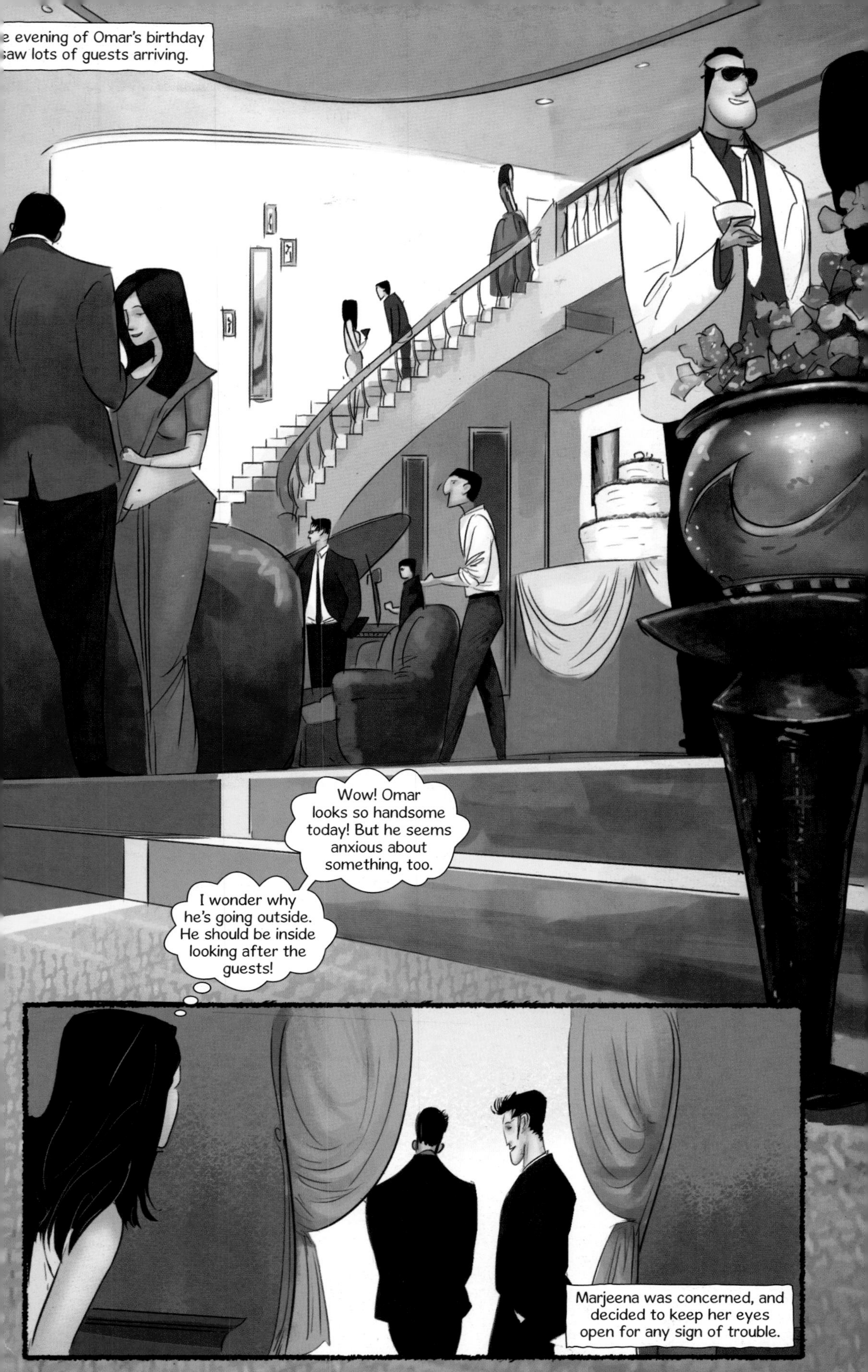
e evening of Omar's birthday
saw lots of guests arriving.
Wow! Omar looks so handsome today! But he seems anxious about something, too.
I wonder why he's going outside. He should be inside looking after the guests!
Marjeena was concerned, and decided to keep her eyes open for any sign of trouble.

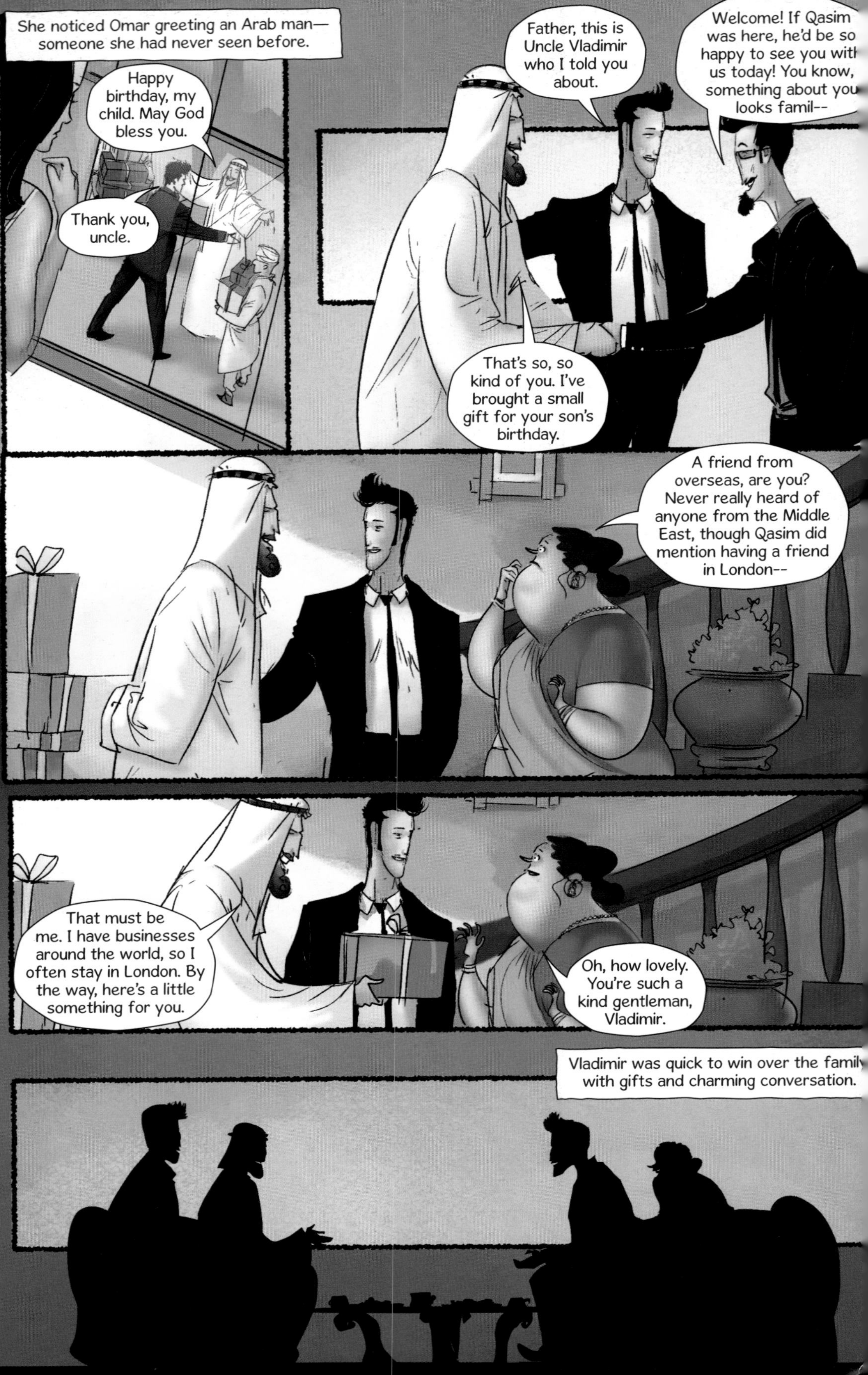
She noticed Omar greeting an Arab man—someone she had never seen before.
Happy birthday, my child. May God bless you.
Thank you, uncle.
Father, this is Uncle Vladimir who I told you about.
Welcome! If Qasim was here, he'd be so happy to see you with us today! You know, something about you looks famil--
That's so, so kind of you. I've brought a small gift for your son's birthday.
A friend from overseas, are you? Never really heard of anyone from the Middle East, though Qasim did mention having a friend in London--
That must be me. I have businesses around the world, so I often stay in London. By the way, here's a little something for you.
Oh, how lovely. You're such a kind gentleman, Vladimir.
Vladimir was quick to win over the family with gifts and charming conversation.

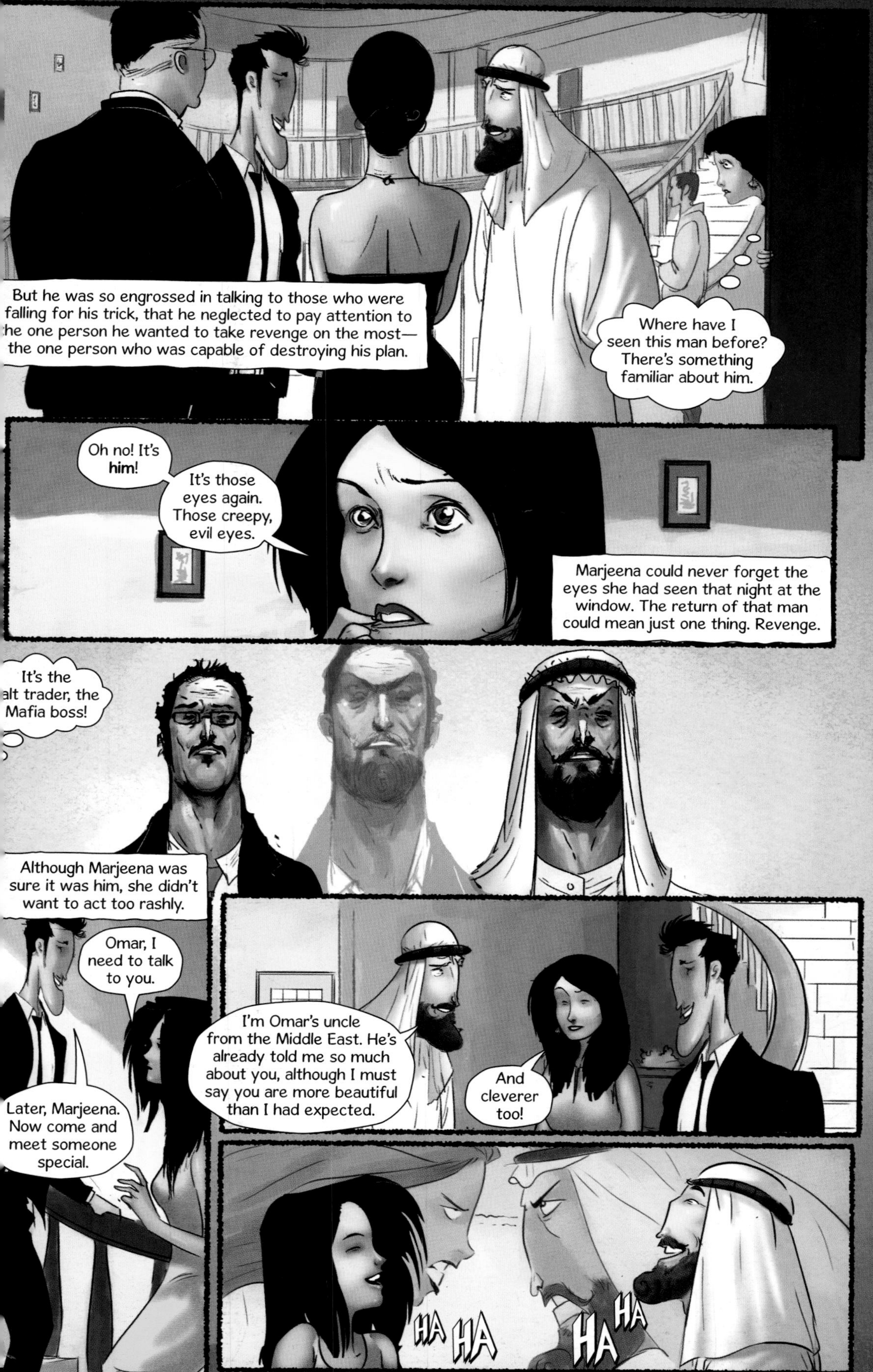

But he was so engrossed in talking to those who were falling for his trick, that he neglected to pay attention to he one person he wanted to take revenge on the most— the one person who was capable of destroying his plan.
Where have I seen this man before? There's something familiar about him.
Oh no! It's **him**!
It's those eyes again. Those creepy, evil eyes.
Marjeena could never forget the eyes she had seen that night at the window. The return of that man could mean just one thing. Revenge.
It's the alt trader, the Mafia boss!
Although Marjeena was sure it was him, she didn't want to act too rashly.
Omar, I need to talk to you.
Later, Marjeena. Now come and meet someone special.
I'm Omar's uncle from the Middle East. He's already told me so much about you, although I must say you are more beautiful than I had expected.
And cleverer too!
HA HA HA HA

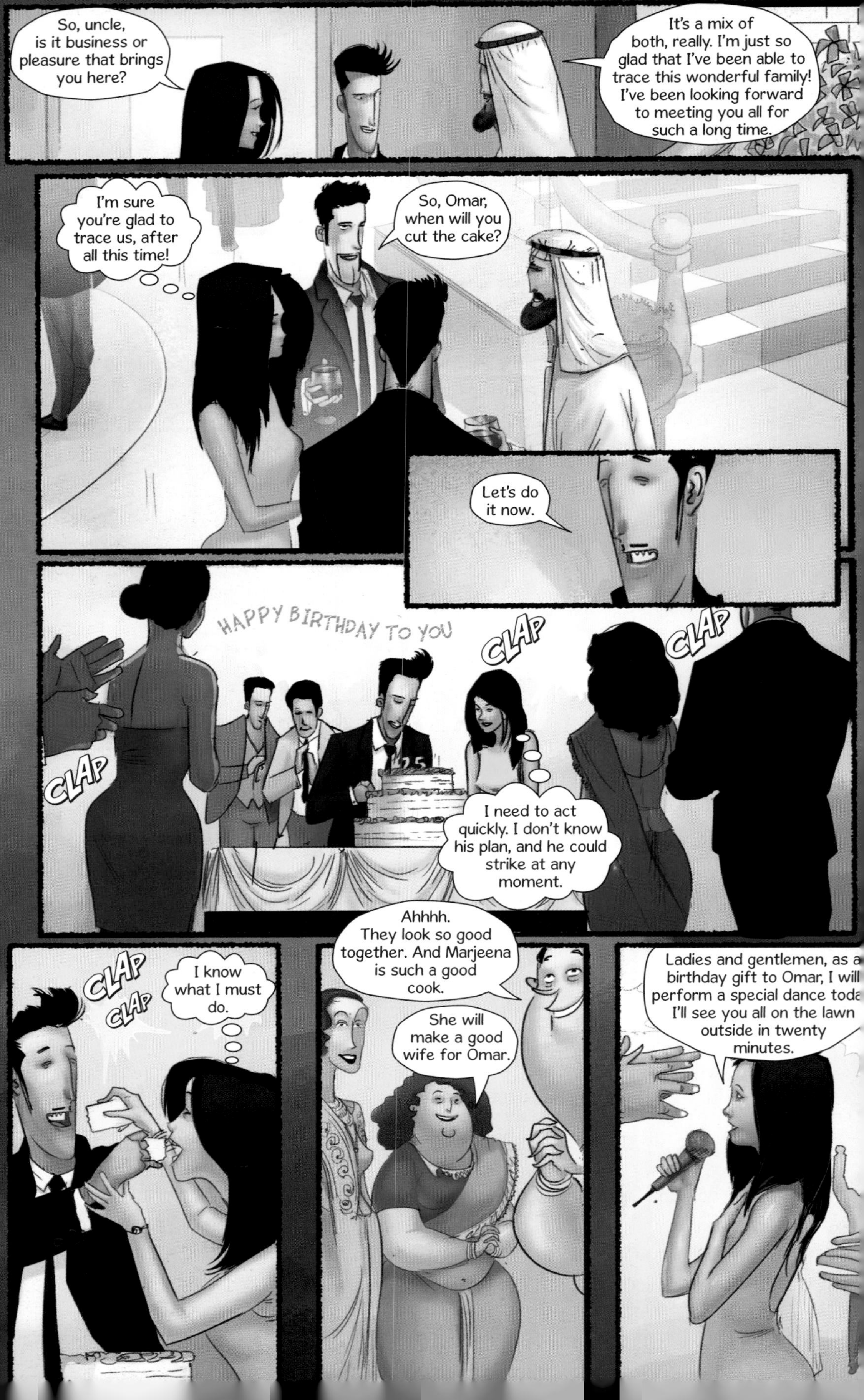

So, uncle, is it business or pleasure that brings you here?
It's a mix of both, really. I'm just so glad that I've been able to trace this wonderful family! I've been looking forward to meeting you all for such a long time.
I'm sure you're glad to trace us, after all this time!
So, Omar, when will you cut the cake?
Let's do it now.
HAPPY BIRTHDAY TO YOU
CLAP
CLAP
CLAP
I need to act quickly. I don't know his plan, and he could strike at any moment.
CLAP
CLAP
I know what I must do.
Ahhhh. They look so good together. And Marjeena is such a good cook.
She will make a good wife for Omar.
Ladies and gentlemen, as a birthday gift to Omar, I will perform a special dance toda
I'll see you all on the lawn outside in twenty minutes.

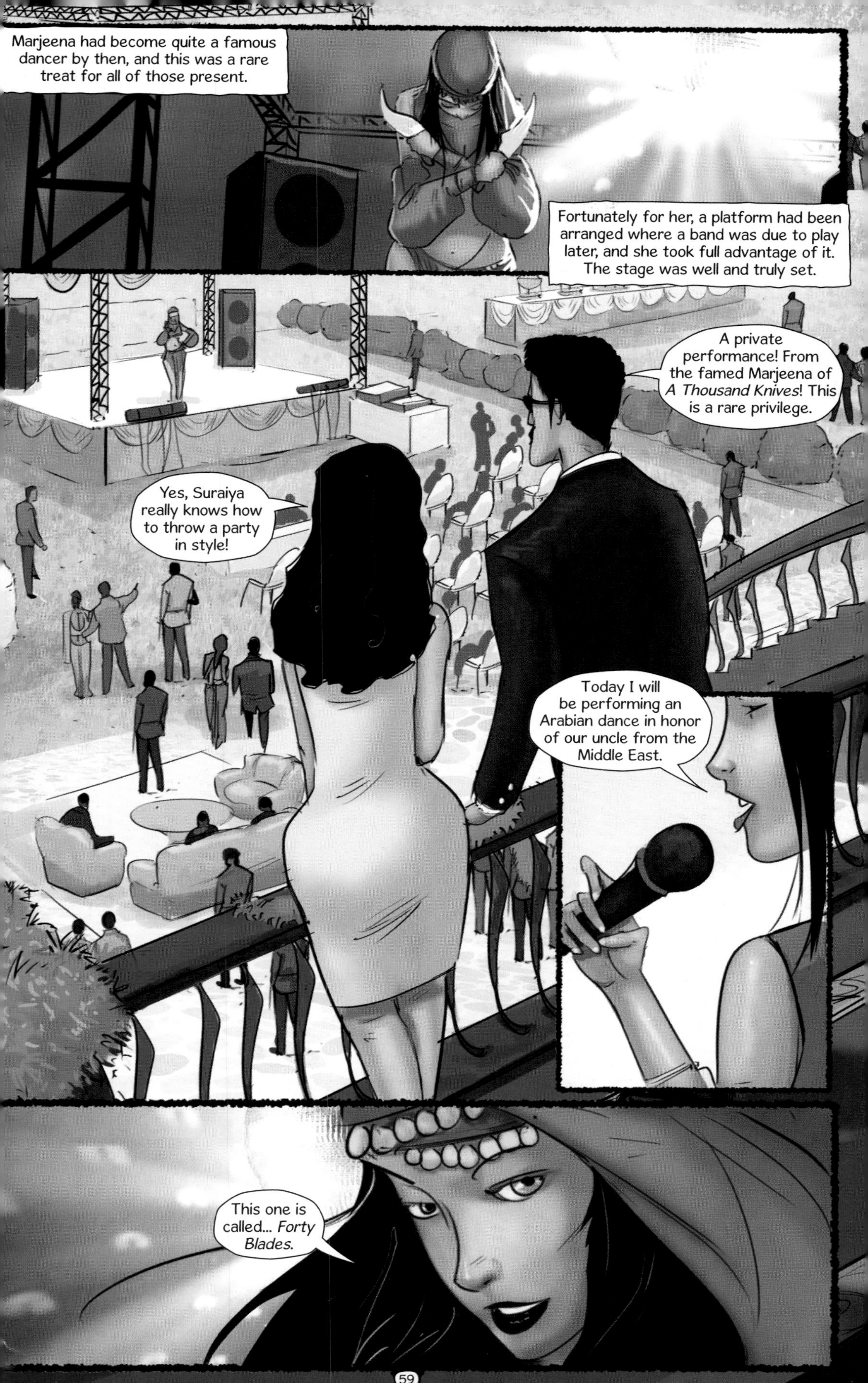
Marjeena had become quite a famous dancer by then, and this was a rare treat for all of those present.
Fortunately for her, a platform had been arranged where a band was due to play later, and she took full advantage of it. The stage was well and truly set.
A private performance! From the famed Marjeena of *A Thousand Knives*! This is a rare privilege.
Yes, Suraiya really knows how to throw a party in style!
Today I will be performing an Arabian dance in honor of our uncle from the Middle East.
This one is called... *Forty Blades*.

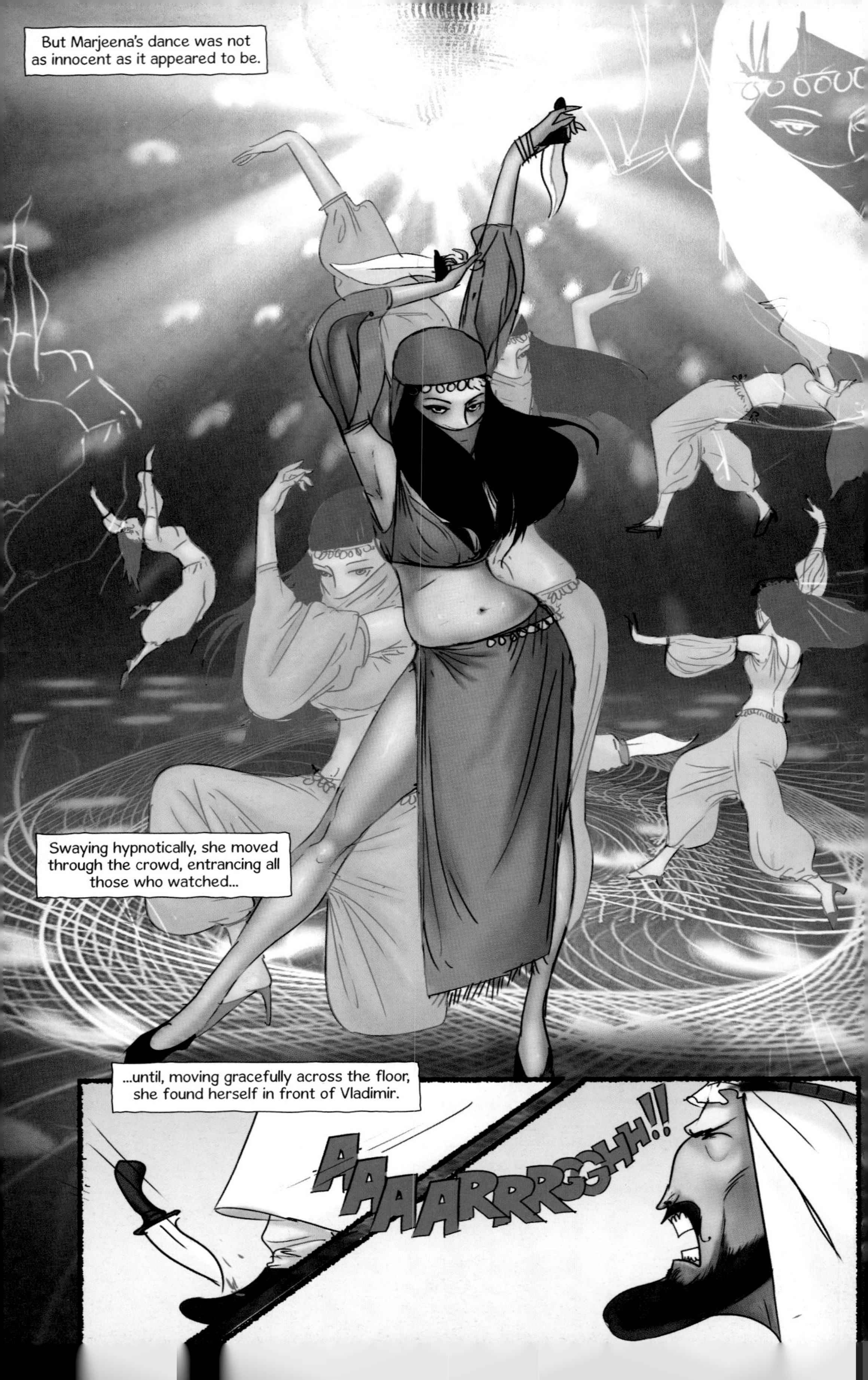
But Marjeena's dance was not as innocent as it appeared to be.
Swaying hypnotically, she moved through the crowd, entrancing all those who watched...
...until, moving gracefully across the floor, she found herself in front of Vladimir.
AAAARRRRGGHH!!

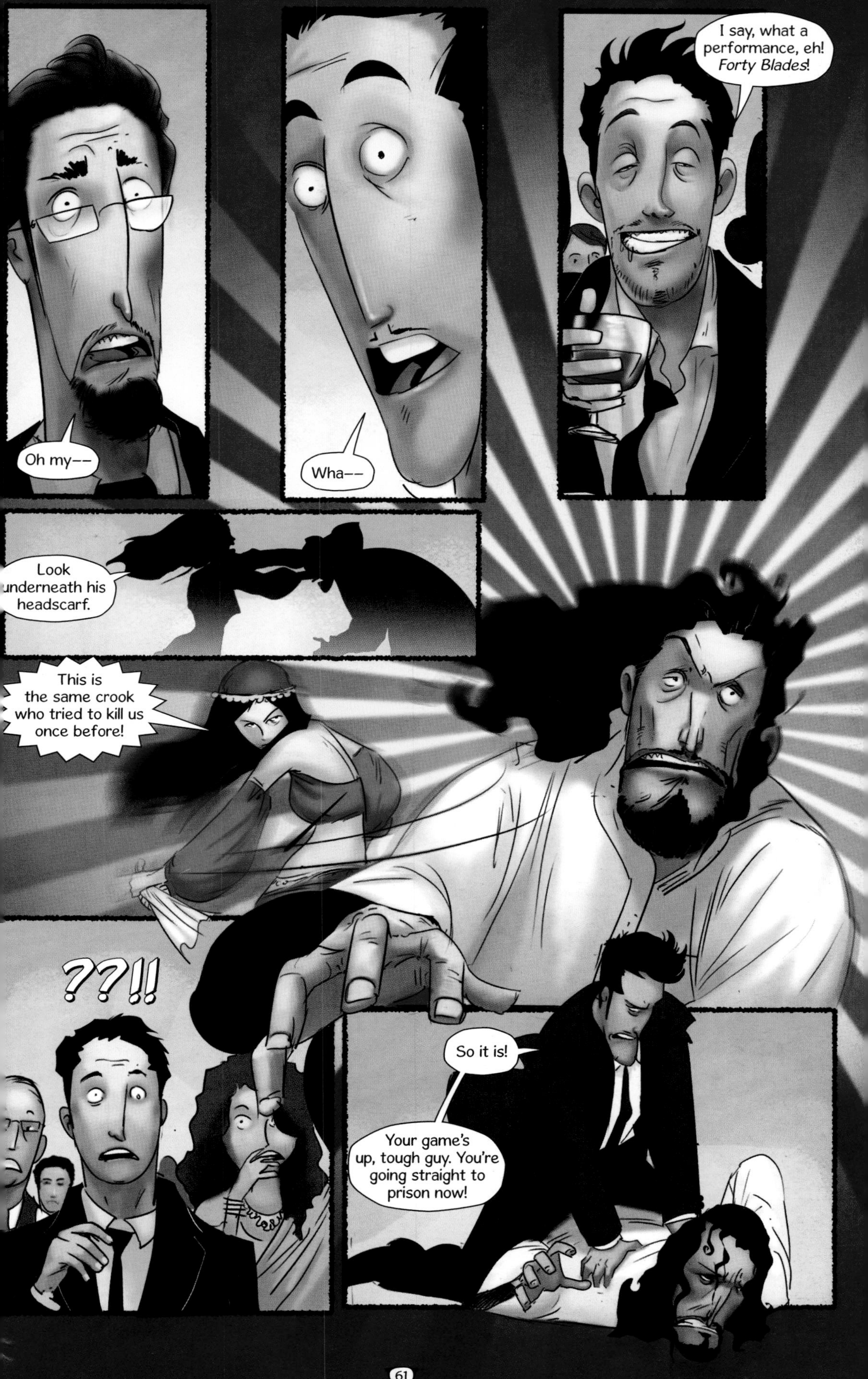
Oh my--
Wha--
I say, what a performance, eh! *Forty Blades*!
Look underneath his headscarf.
This is the same crook who tried to kill us once before!
??!!
So it is!
Your game's up, tough guy. You're going straight to prison now!

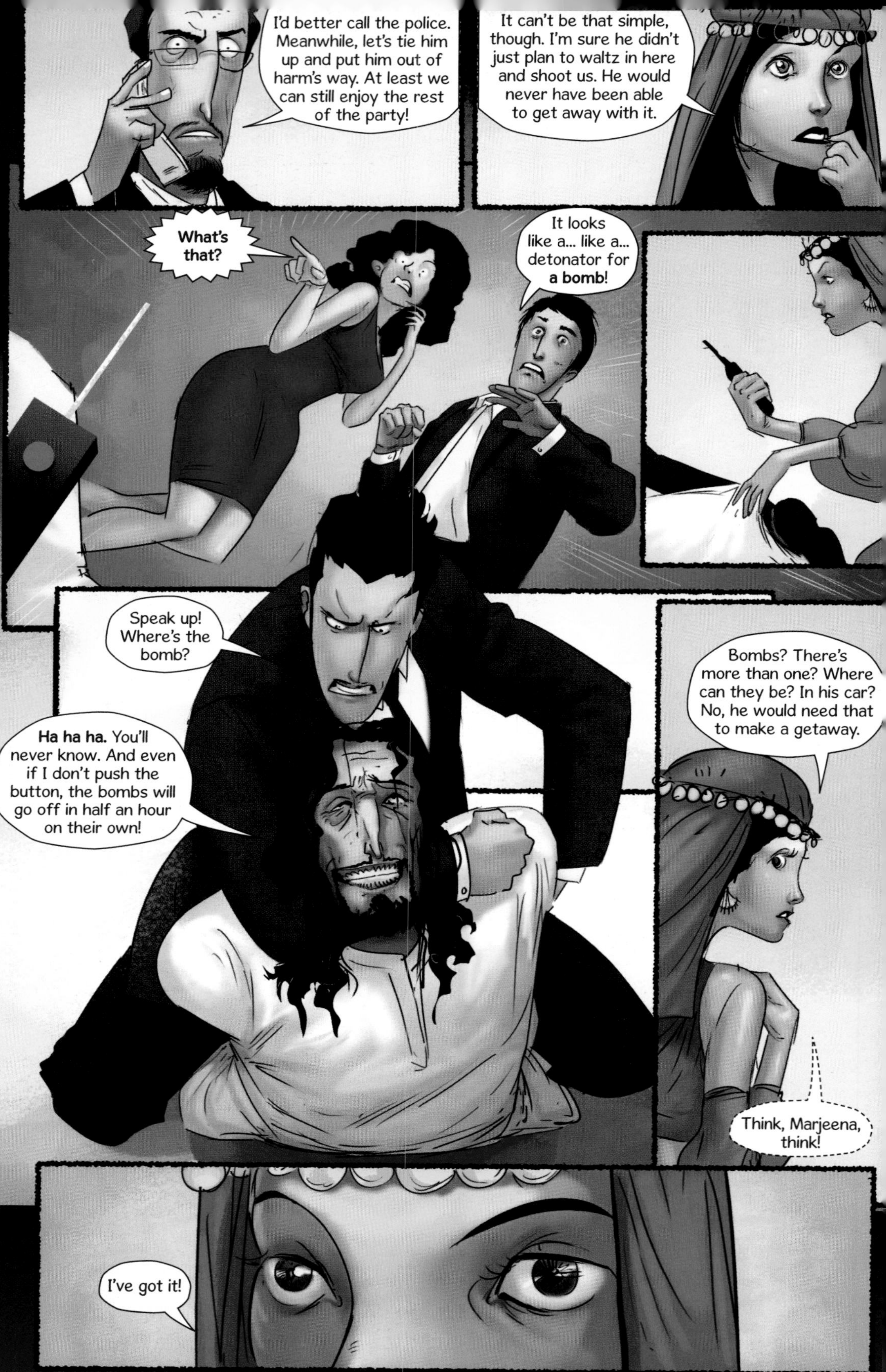
I'd better call the police. Meanwhile, let's tie him up and put him out of harm's way. At least we can still enjoy the rest of the party!
It can't be that simple, though. I'm sure he didn't just plan to waltz in here and shoot us. He would never have been able to get away with it.
What's that?
It looks like a... like a... detonator for a bomb!
Speak up! Where's the bomb?
Ha ha ha. You'll never know. And even if I don't push the button, the bombs will go off in half an hour on their own!
Bombs? There's more than one? Where can they be? In his car? No, he would need that to make a getaway.
Think, Marjeena, think!
I've got it!

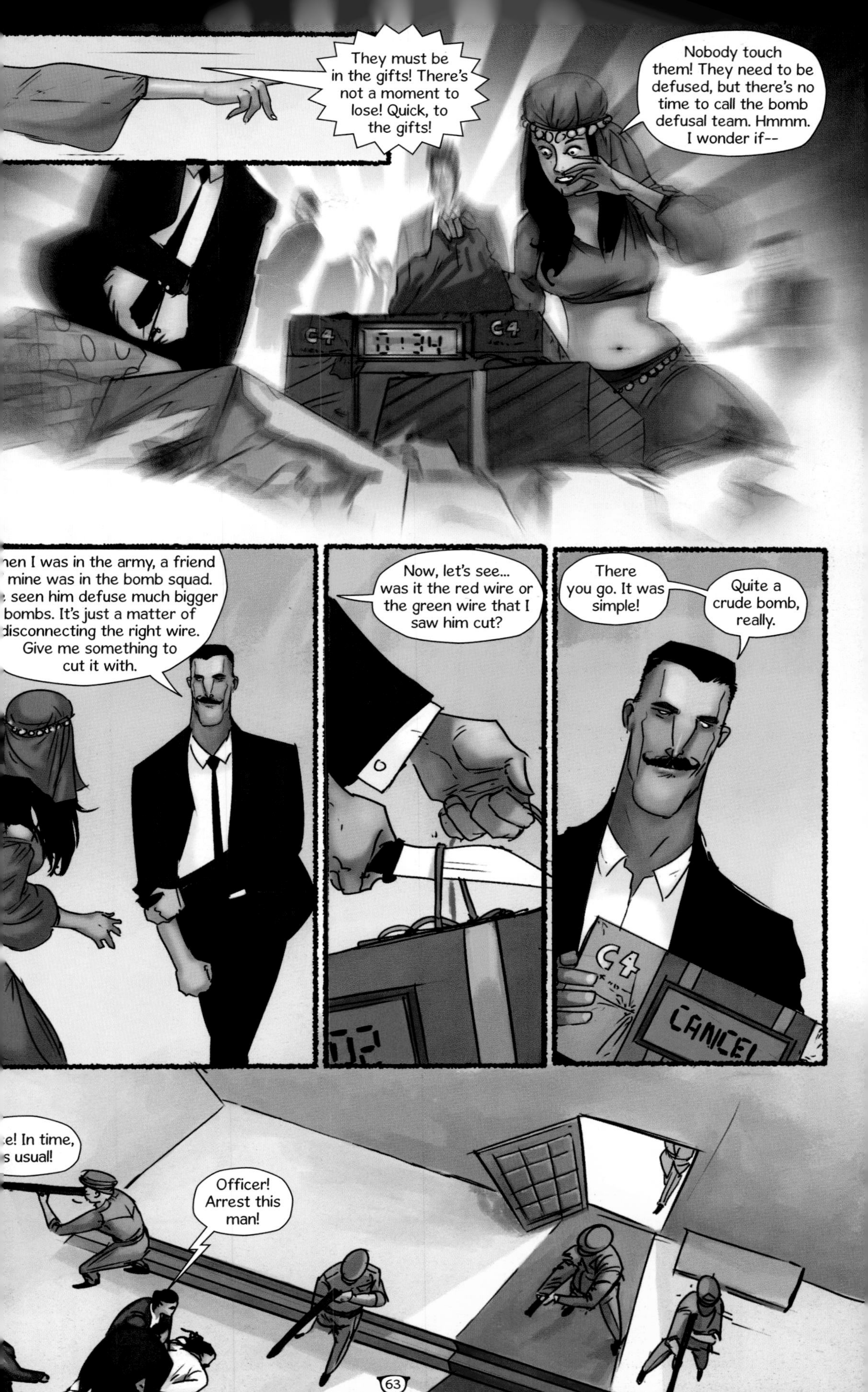
They must be in the gifts! There's not a moment to lose! Quick, to the gifts!
Nobody touch them! They need to be defused, but there's no time to call the bomb defusal team. Hmmm. I wonder if--
C4
C4
nen I was in the army, a friend mine was in the bomb squad. seen him defuse much bigger bombs. It's just a matter of disconnecting the right wire. Give me something to cut it with.
Now, let's see... was it the red wire or the green wire that I saw him cut?
There you go. It was simple!
Quite a crude bomb, really.
C4
CANCEL
e! In time, s usual!
Officer! Arrest this man!

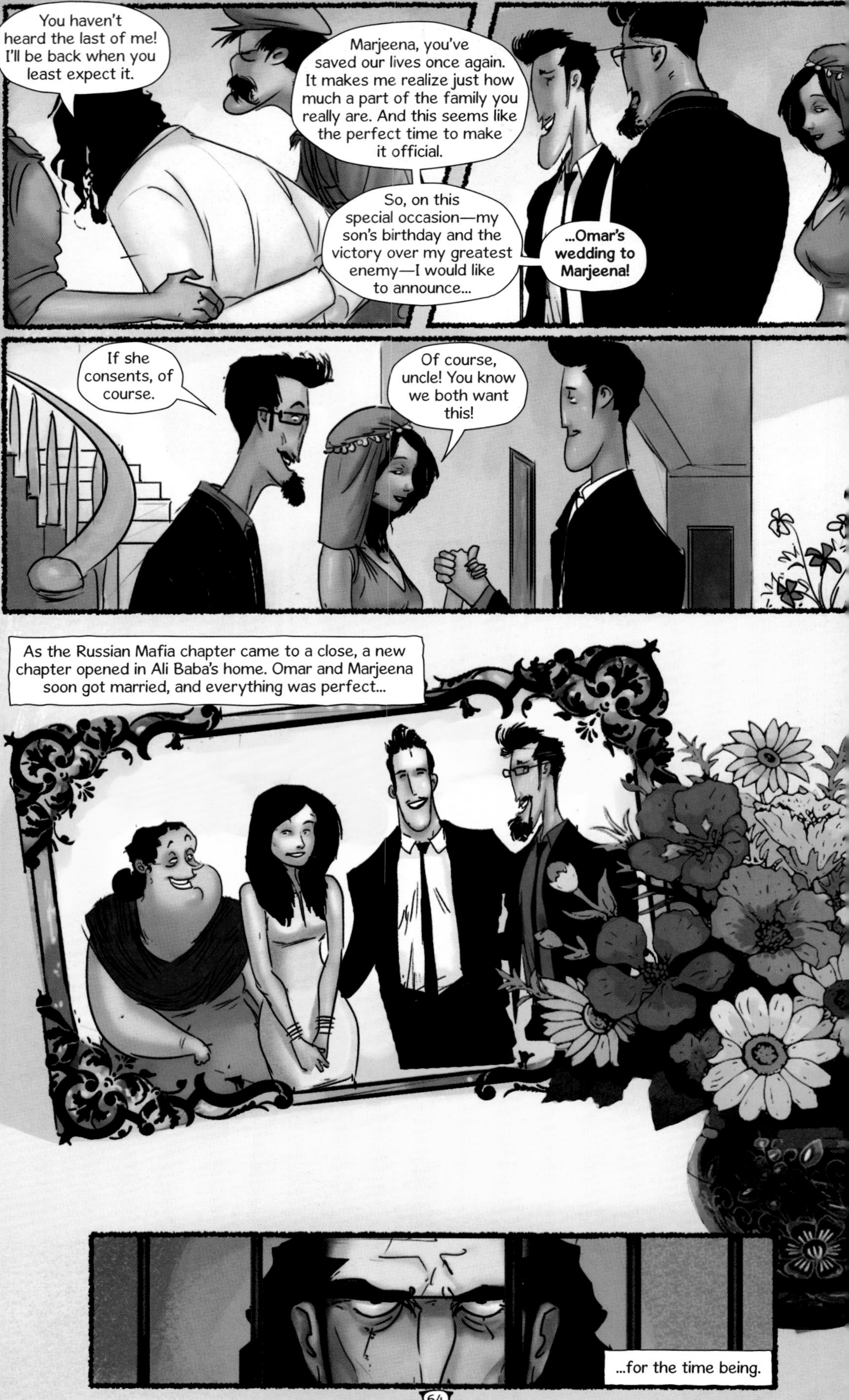
You haven't heard the last of me! I'll be back when you least expect it.
Marjeena, you've saved our lives once again. It makes me realize just how much a part of the family you really are. And this seems like the perfect time to make it official.
So, on this special occasion—my son's birthday and the victory over my greatest enemy—I would like to announce...
...Omar's wedding to Marjeena!
If she consents, of course.
Of course, uncle! You know we both want this!
As the Russian Mafia chapter came to a close, a new chapter opened in Ali Baba's home. Omar and Marjeena soon got married, and everything was perfect...
...for the time being.

POULOMI MUKHERJEE

Poulomi was born in the steel city of Jamshedpur, India and spent her formative years there. Bedtime stories spurred her imagination while folklore and mythological stories provided inspiration. Soon she was spinning her own world of characters, which were first put on paper for 'Voices' in *The Statesman*, a national daily newspaper.

Poulomi's curious mind found a new avenue when she discovered the world of advertising. Advertisements told a story, but the medium was new and different. This gave her the impetus to go against her parents' wish of seeing her graduate from medical school, and she set forth to pursue a more creative career. From a copywriter in advertising agencies to a brand manager, she continued to meet new challenges every day.

After six years of successfully connecting people to brands, Poulomi discovered something different but just as wonderful: travel writing. Here was something that allowed her to indulge in the two things she was so passionate about: traveling and writing. Presently, as well as writing for Campfire, she is associated with a leading media group and moonlights as an avid travel blogger. And if this is not enough, she is penning a travel book too.

FOLK LITERATURE AND THE ARABIAN NIGHTS

The story you just read is an adaptation of the original *Ali Baba and the Forty Thieves*. It is part of a larger collection of 1001 stories, together known as *The Arabian Nights*. These stories are said to have originated in Persia, now Iran, and are a part of their folk literature.

WHAT IS FOLK LITERATURE?

Once upon a time, when language was young, tales were passed down orally through generations. Traditional knowledge and beliefs had no written script. This legacy is what we now know as folk literature. It consists of stories and poems, just like any written literature does.

Now that we know what folk literature is all about, let's find out more about *The Arabian Nights*.

* According to a popular Arabian belief, anyone who reads all the 1001 stories of *The Arabian Nights* will go mad!

* *The Arabian Nights* inspired Russian composer Nikolai Rimsky-Korsakov to write the nationalistic symphonic suite *Scheherazade*.

* For hundreds of years, these tales were kept alive by word of mouth. It was only in around 1400 A.D. that Egyptian scholars began to collect and compile them. A popular compilation of these stories is by Antoine Galland who wrote the first European translation of the tales in 1704 A.D.

Influences on *The Arabian Nights*

The Arabian Nights has been significantly influenced by various cultures and elements. Many of the animal stories in *The Arabian Nights* find a parallel in Indian folklore like the famous *Panchatantra* and *Jataka Tales*. The stories also seem to have taken ideas from medieval Egyptian, Persian, and Jewish folklore. Stylistically too, there are similarities to be found. *The Arabian Nights* uses the 'frame story', a literary technique that dates back to ancient Indian literature. It was used in the *Panchatantra* stories and was later adopted in Persian and Arabic Literature.

Frame Story of *The Arabian Nights*

Distraught to find that his wife was unfaithful to him, King Shahryar married a girl every night and killed her the next morning. Every young girl in the kingdom lived in fear till the king's minister's daughter, Sheherazade, made up her mind to marry the king. After the marriage, she intrigued the king in a manner no one ever had. She would weave a series of stories, withholding the climax of each story till the following night. Eager to know what would happen next, the king would postpone her execution to the following day.

This continued for a thousand and one nights, at the end of which the king realized that he was in love with his wise wife. He gave up his wicked ways and they lived happily ever after. Thus, within this framework or 'frame story', many other stories were told.

WHERE DO YOU THINK GENIES, FLYING CARPETS, AND MAGIC LAMPS CAME FROM?

No prizes for guessing! Yes, *The Arabian Nights*! So popular is *The Arabian Nights* that many characters like Aladdin, Sinbad, and Ali Baba have become popular cultural icons in the Western world. Magical elements like genies, magic lamps, and flying carpets have become a part of modern fantasy too.

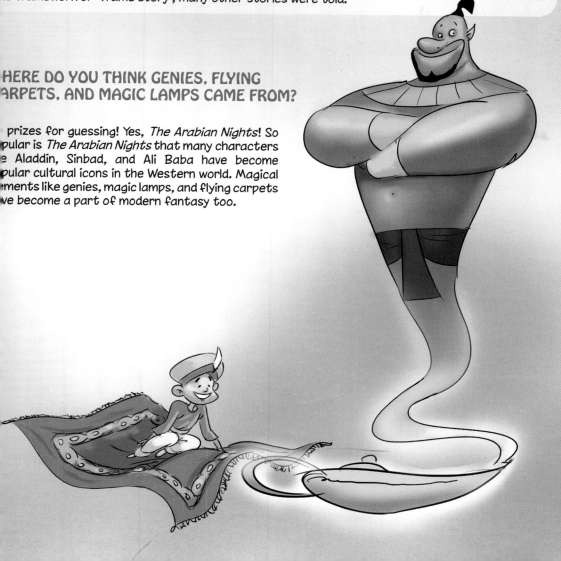

Available now

Putting the fun back into reading!